# MARRIED TO THE BOSS OF ATLANTA

## DANI LITTLEPAGE

Cole Hart
SIGNATURE NOVELS

**Married To The Boss Of Atlanta**

**Mailing List**

To stay up to date on new releases, plus get information on contests, sneak peeks, and more,

*Go To The Website Below...*

www.colehartsignature.com

# 1

The Atlanta Convention center was packed with beautiful women who were all well-dressed. Most of them were coupled up and being escorted by their husbands. Tuxedos, bowties and roses were the dress code for most of them. Camilla sat at a decorated table. She had a wide grin spread across her face as she listened to her husband of four years give his acceptance speech for winning the businessman of the year award for the second year in a row. She gazed in admiration at how handsome her husband, Kane, looked in his black tailored Armani suit with his fresh Caesar fade, neatly trimmed mustache and goatee and glowing brown skin. Camilla was finding it hard to contain the sexual urges that were flowing through her body. With her focus still on Kane, she felt a sharp pain in her knee and quickly glanced in her three-year-old son's direction.

"Sorry, mama but this is taking too long, and I'm bored," her son, Kannon, whined.

"Hush that whining, child, and act like you got some manners," Camilla's mother, Maggie, whispered in her grandson's ear.

Folding his arms over his chest, Kannon pouted quietly and listened to the rest of his father's speech.

"In closing, I would like to say that I wouldn't be where I am today if it wasn't for my wonderful and beautiful wife encouraging and supporting me every step of the way," Kane smiled, "Stand up so everyone can see you."

Slightly embarrassed, Camilla stood to her feet and blew a kiss to her husband as the crowded room erupted in applause. As Kane stepped from behind the podium with his trophy in hand, she watched as her husband shook hands with the other nominees for the award on his way back to their table. Wrapping her arms around his neck, Camilla softly kissed his lips before tightly embracing him.

"I'm so proud of you bae," she cooed.

"You know I meant everything I said." Kane broke their embrace. "I wouldn't be where I am without you Camilla. I love you so much."

"I love you too, Kane." She smiled.

As the family congratulated him on his victory, Kannon lifted his arms for his father to pick him up and Kane obliged. After mingling with the guests for a few minutes and taking a few couple and family photos, Camilla and Kane said their goodbyes to her parents and hopped inside their cars once valet arrived. Kane opened the door for her before strapping their son in his car seat. Closing the passenger door, she leaned over to open the door for her husband. When Kane was comfortable behind the wheel of his gun-metal grey 2019 Mercedes-Benz, he pulled off and drove to their seven bedroom, thirteen-bathroom mansion in Atlanta. Camilla nodded her head to the music as Kane's hand grabbed hers freeing her from her thoughts.

"I am so glad this night is over." He loosened his tie keeping his focus on the road. "I was nervous as hell standing up there."

"Well, I couldn't tell. You were the three C's up there, and I couldn't stop thinking about how sexy you look in that suit." Camilla seductively smiled.

"Thank you, baby." Kane grinned. "You're looking sexy as hell yourself. Every time I have you on my arm, the men just stare at you and the women instantly become uncomfortable in your presence. You are one dangerous woman, Camilla Jacobs."

"I wouldn't say all that." She downplayed his comment. "But I will say that you make me feel like I'm the most beautiful woman in the world."

"That's because you are." Kane kissed her hand, sending chills through her body.

With her hand still in his, the couple made small talk the rest of the way home. During their conversation, she began massaging Kane's dick through his dress pants, making it hard for him to keep his focus on the road. Camilla kept an eye on their sleeping son to ensure that he didn't catch her feeling up on his dad. Her pussy was dripping wet, and she was ready to ride her husband until they both fell asleep. As Kane pulled into their gated driveway minutes later, Camilla didn't wait for Kane to put the car in park before she jumped out, which caused him to chuckle. Removing Kannon from his car seat, the sound of Kane's phone ringing changed her mood immediately.

"Baby, don't answer that," she spoke irritably.

"Camilla, I have to take this. It's my father, and you know he wouldn't be calling me at this hour if it wasn't important," Kane replied.

"Fine."

Slamming the door shut, she stormed towards the front door with her son on her hip. Camilla let herself in and marched up the staircase to Kannon's room where she turned on his night light removing his suit and dress shoes. Once his PJ Mask pajamas were on, she tucked him in, kissed his forehead, left the room, and headed to her own. With the lights turning on when Camilla entered their large master bedroom, she strolled over to the walk-in closet and began to undress.

"Camilla!" Kane shouted from down stairs.

"What!" She answered sharply, dragging herself to the hallway, and looking over the railing.

"My pops wants to holla at me about something important, and it can't wait until morning. I'll be back in a few hours, aight?"

"Whatever, Kane." Camilla rolled her eyes.

"Look, I know you horny and wanted to spend the evening with me, but I need you to kill the fucking attitude," Kane sternly spoke. "I told you this shit was important and couldn't wait. So fix your fucking attitude, let me handle my business, and when I get back, I'll give you all the dick you want. Aight?"

"Kane you always do this—"

"I don't give a fuck about nothing you gotta say right now," he cut her off. "All I wanna hear is 'yes daddy'."

"Yes, Daddy," Camilla mumbled.

Glaring at her for a moment, Kane walked out the door slamming it shut. Camilla walked slowly down the hallway back to their master bedroom with her head down to the floor. She hated when Kane shut her down and talked to her like she was a child. After being married to him for four years, Camilla had gotten used to most of her husband's rude, arrogant, and male chauvinistic ways, but being disrespected and talked down to was not one of them. Many times, she wanted to put Kane's ass in his place, but feared the consequences. So, instead of speaking up for herself, Camilla learned to bite her tongue. Every time she allowed him to disrespect her, she felt apart of herself die but in order for her to keep her husband and continue living the good life, Camilla felt that it was a small price to pay.

At the age of seventeen, Camilla's parents, Maggie and Richard, introduced her to Kane and his father Karl. Camilla didn't pay any attention to Kane the entire time he was in her presence but once her parents insisted that she became more acquainted with the twenty-one-year-old boy, Camilla decided to give him a chance, and she slowly found herself falling in love with Kane. She loved being wined, dined, and spoiled by the older gentleman, and while they were dating, he never disrespected her. Kane valued her opinion and always listened to what she had to say but when they got married when Camilla was eighteen, Kane slowly started showing his true colors. The loving, caring, understanding and considerate man she fell in love with turned into a control freak and a dictator. In their first year of marriage, Camilla complained to her mother about his behavior, hoping that she would give her some useful advice. But when Maggie told her to just be a good little wife and do whatever Kane said, Camilla was stunned by her words because her mother raised her to speak up for herself, demand respect, and to have a mind of her own. Instead of arguing with her mother, Camilla followed her advice and that was how she'd been living her life since then.

When Camilla reached her room, she put on her Tory Lanez 'I Told You' album then grabbed her iPad where she checked her emails, scrolled through social media, and played games until she became tired. Placing her iPad back on the nightstand, Camilla was getting comfortable in her bed when she received a text from Kane. A part of her wanted to ignore him, but she never could leave her husband on read, even if she was mad. Snatching her phone from the nightstand, Camilla unlocked her phone and read it.

**Kane: I apologize for the way I treated you before I left. You didn't deserve that and I promise that I'm gonna do a better job of working on my temper and try not to be so controlling. I love you Camilla.**

**Camilla: I love you too Kane and I hope you do.**

Placing her phone down next to her, Camilla silently prayed

that her husband kept his promise to her. There was no doubt that she loved Kane. She just wanted him to turn back into the man she fell in love with. Even though Camilla knew that it was going to take some time for Kane to change his ways, she hoped that he would show some improvements soon because she was growing tired of the disrespect and mistreatment.

## 2

With his eyes still glued to his phone, Kane reread Camilla's response to his text, tuning out the conversation that was going on around him. Replaying the conversation they had before he left the house, he couldn't help but feel like shit for the way he treated his wife. All Camilla wanted was to spend time with him and end the night on a high note with some mind-blowing sex but, like always, he put his father, business and everything else before her and expected her to deal with the last-minute shit that came up and not be upset. Knowing that Camilla had every right to be disappointed with him, Kane never took the high road and apologized for having to cut their plans short. Instead, he just shut her down, told her to get out of her feelings and left without a second thought. Although he was aware of his rude behavior, Kane never thought that his poor manners would cause Camilla to leave him. He was damn certain that the love she had for him was strong enough to stand the test of time, but he knew that sooner or later his wife was going to grow tired of him dismissing and mistreating her. Kane was aware that he needed to change his ways but after twenty-five years of being an asshole, he wasn't sure if he could.

"Kane! Are you paying attention?" His father, Karl, shouted, bringing him back to reality.

"I'm sorry, sir." He stuffed his phone in his pocket. "My mind was somewhere else."

"No shit. Now get your head outta the damn clouds and listen." Karl glared at him.

Sitting up straight in his chair, Kane gave his father and father-in-law his undivided attention.

"Like I was saying," Richard continued. "Now that our computer software is circulating throughout most of Atlanta, we need to focus on our expansion project. I already have a meeting set up with some folks in Alabama next week, but I think we should start setting up meetings with some of the big wigs up North."

"I agree," Karl chimed in. "We're not just trying to be known in the south but all over the world."

"I'm glad that we're all on the same page gentleman and as you know, I always stay one step ahead of the game," Kane bragged. "I have three meetings set up in Maryland, New York and Philadelphia. I can do the meetings in NY and Philly but I'm not gonna be able to do the one in Maryland."

"I'll go to Maryland. I love to visit that harbor whenever I visit." Karl volunteered.

"Well gentlemen, if there is nothing else to discuss, I'm gonna head on out. Maggie was pissed that I had to leave her to attend this emergency meeting." Richard stood to his feet.

Shaking their hands before making his exit, Kane poured himself a drink as he waited for his father to return from walking Richard to the door. He took a huge sip of the Tequila allowing the sting of the alcohol to burn his chest on the way down. Kane sat back down in his chair as his thoughts shifted back to Camilla.

"So, do you care to tell me what caused you to zone out during our meeting with Richard?" Karl questioned entering his office.

"I was thinking about Camilla," he sighed, "I think she might be getting tired of me."

"What the hell did you do now, Kane?" his father glared at him.

"She got upset because I had to cut our evening short, so I could attend the meeting. I told her to stop being childish and let me handle my business. Every time a call comes through about business, I toss whatever plans I have with my wife to the side and rush off. I didn't realize how she comes second to everything until now."

Watching his father shake his head, Kane downed his drink to prepare himself for his father's response.

"Son, I told you years ago that you weren't ready to be married but you insisted that Camilla was the woman you wanted to be with. You looked me in my eyes and promised me that you would take care of and do right by my best friend's daughter. Hell, I even convinced her parents that Camilla would be in good hands with you but every time you tell me some shit like this, you make me regret my decision for allowing you to accept her hand in marriage," Karl boldly spoke, "Richard and I have been friends and business partners for over twenty-five years, and I'll be damned if that comes to an end because your ignorant ass don't know how to treat your wife! Hear me and hear me good Kane, you better do whatever it takes to keep that girl happy. I don't care if she asks for the damn moon, you better figure out a way to give it to her. Do you understand me?"

"Yes, sir," he quickly responded.

"Now get your ass outta my office and go make things right with Camilla."

Without speaking another word, Kane rose to his feet,

placed his empty glass on his desk and strolled out of his father's office with his feelings hurt. Unlocking the doors to his car, he jumped inside, started the engine and pulled out of the long driveway. As he headed towards the expressway, Kane was confused as to how he was supposed to make his wife happy when he didn't know how. Although he'd dated quite a few women before settling down with Camilla, he didn't care about what they liked, wanted or needed. All they were good for was a nut, and once Kane busted his, it was on to the next, but after being married for four years and with no help from the parental figures in his life, Kane was clueless as to what he needed to do to have a successful and happy marriage.

Thinking back to when he first started dating Camilla, Kane found himself smiling at the things they used to do and how much fun they used to have. The countless trips they used to take, the fine dining experiences they encountered along with the expensive gifts he bought for her caused a warm feeling to enter his heart and an idea entered his head. With his thoughts racing a mile a minute, Kane got excited as he thought about all the things he wanted to do for his wife. Taking his father's advice, he was going to do whatever he needed to do to make Camilla happy. He needed to prove to himself and Karl that he could be the husband he promised he would be, and he wasn't going to let himself or his parental figures down.

# 3

9 *1...92....93*
Rafiq silently counted off the number of sit-ups in his head as the sweat poured down his face. The pain that he was feeling in his abdominal area would have made an average person tap out, but Rafiq pushed past the pain until he reached a hundred. Embracing the pain of his work out, he got into the push- up position and began his set of a hundred. The hard, cold floor of the Fulton County Jail had his hands feeling numb, but he was so in tune with his workout that it didn't even bother him. After finishing his morning routine, Rafiq jumped to his feet, grabbing the white towel from his cot and wiped his face with it before letting out a long sigh. He looked at the letter on his bed that he had been reading all night that had him filled with anticipation. The letter that Rafiq had received two weeks prior from his favorite cousin stated that he would be paying him a visit that day and he could not wait to see him. It had been a few months since he had any visitors, and he was looking forward to seeing him.

After waiting nearly an hour for the officers to unlock his cell, Rafiq gathered the things he needed and headed towards the showers. He was always one of the first inmates to wash because he wasn't with that sharing showers shit. Once he was finished, he quickly put on his jumpsuit and headed back to his cell where he finished the rest of his grooming process. Rafiq put on one of his favorite oil scents before examining himself in the mirror over his sink. With a cocky smile on his face, he rubbed his hands together giving himself the stamp of approval. With deep waves in his fade, almond-shaped brown eyes, a baby face, and a bright smile, as well as milk chocolate skin, Rafiq knew he was that nigga. The male officers and some of the inmates hated his ass, but the female officers loved him and even though he never gave them the time of day, they were all more than willing to fulfill whatever needs he might have.

"Sanders! You got a visit!" The husky male officer called out.

Without saying a word, Rafiq turned around and followed the officer to the visiting area where they searched him before allowing him to go inside. Scanning the visiting room, he spotted his cousin sitting at one of the tables in the back. Once he handed guard his I.D pass, Rafiq made his way over to him.

"Wassup, nigga?" His cousin, Boyce, greeted him with a smile.

"Same shit different day, my nigga." Rafiq returned the smile.

"I hear that, man," Boyce nodded.

The men exchanged a quick bro hug before sitting down at the table.

"So what's new with you? It's been a while since we talked." Boyce folded his hands on the table.

"I should be asking you that question since I haven't heard from you in three months," Rafiq responded in a serious tone.

"I apologize for that, man, but I had some shit I needed to handle with my mom." Boyce dropped his head. "The day after I came to visit you, I got a call from my mom's next-door neighbor saying that she heard some commotion coming from her house and that she had called the police. When I got there, the police had the street blocked off, and they weren't trying to let me through, but after I bullied my way past them... I saw that my mom was dead." He sniffled. "Somebody killed my mom, Fiq."

Hearing that his favorite aunt was murdered caused Rafiq's heart to ache instantly. His aunt Jackie was the woman that took him in and raised him after his mother ran out on him when he was only seven years old. Although he was her nephew, his aunt Jackie treated him like her son and made sure Rafiq was well cared for just like she did for her own three children. When he got locked up at the age of eighteen, his aunt always came to visit him when she could and made sure that he had more than enough money on his books. Rafiq thought about all the things he promised his aunt that he was going to do when he was released. The trips that they were going to take and the new house that he was going to put her in were a couple of the promises he made, and it was killing him that he was not going to be able to deliver on his promises because someone killed her.

After taking a few moments to process his thoughts, Rafiq's pain instantly turned to anger.

"This shit doesn't make any sense man." He shook his head in disbelief. "Why would someone kill Aunt Jackie? All she does is go to work, mind her business and chill. Why the fuck would someone kill her!" He slammed his fist down on the table drawing the attention of the people around them.

"At first I was just as confused as you were bro." Boyce lifted his head. "But after searching her house for answers, I think I know why she was killed."

"Wassup?" Rafiq leaned forward anxious to hear his cousin's theory.

"I found some documents at her house from a lawyer's office about reopening your case because you were falsely accused of a crime you didn't commit. The lawyer agreed to look over your case and he said that he would notify her if he had anything. Two weeks after she was killed, a letter came from the law firm saying that after reviewing everything, they agreed to retrial your case. Since then I've been working with lawyers on trying to get you outta here, but I believe that whoever framed you found out that my mom was trying to get you outta jail and to stop her from doing so, they killed her," Boyce spoke through gritted teeth.

"The last time I saw her, she did say that she was going to do something about getting me outta here. I asked her what her plan was, but she never told me. She just told me to trust her. If I woulda known that this was going to be the end result of her helping me, I woulda talked her out of doing it." His eyes filled with tears.

"Aye, bro. Don't blame yaself for this shit. You know my mom loved you like a son, and you know she wasn't gonna let you rot in here for something that you didn't do. And you better believe that her death will be avenged," Boyce uplifted his cousin. "But first, we're gonna focus on getting you outta here, and once we do that, we'll take care of the rest. Aight?"

"Aight." Rafiq quickly wiped the tears from his eyes. "How's your wife handling everything?"

"Nakia is doing better than I am," he chuckled. "When I first told her about, she was devastated. She was fucked up about it for a month but like the soldier she is, she pulled herself together and got back into the swing of things. You know Nakia has a soft spot for my mom and she is more than ready to fuck someone up for answers."

"Yeah. I bet," he laughed. "Nakia was always ready to pop off at any given moment. I remember when we used to go out with her and her friend and how they fought damn near any bitch that came near us."

"Hell yeah!" Boyce went into a fit of laughter, "Her friend

was hella protective over you too. She used to flip the fuck out whenever she saw you with another bitch and y'all weren't even dating or fucking."

Their laughter continued.

"Yeah. Those were the days." Rafiq brought his laughter to an end. "Whatever happened to shawty? Are Nakia and her friend still cool?"

"Nah. The last time we saw shawty, was the last time we all hung out together when we were teenagers. Nakia said shawty got into some serious trouble that night with her parents and they ended her friendship with Nakia. They haven't seen each other since but Nakia hasn't forgotten about her. She still has all the pictures they had taken together and it's not a day that passes when she doesn't look at them. Camilla is still my wife's best friend."

"It's fucked up how shawty's parents kept her on a tight leash. I always considered her to be a stuck-up rich kid but once I got to know her, she was cool as fuck." Rafiq smiled.

As they continued to reminisce about the past, Rafiq shared a lot of laughs with his cousin making their visit an enjoyable one. When their visit was over, they embraced each other in a hug and Boyce promised to come see him again in a couple of weeks. Rafiq told him that he would call him soon before his cousin left out of the visiting room. Picking up his pass from the counter, he headed out the visiting room and was escorted back to his cell where he got comfortable on his cot and watched TV. Thinking back to the conversation he had about his childhood and Camilla brought back a lot of memories. Throughout the six years that he had been in jail, Rafiq buried a lot of his feelings and memories about his childhood, because it hurt too much to think about them and Camilla was a part of that. Whenever he would recall the times that they spent with each other, Rafiq found himself daydreaming about her and what she was doing with her life. He sometimes wondered why he had not heard from her but after learning that her parents cut her friendship with Nakia short, he had his answer. Although he considered Camilla to be a stuck-up rich kid, Rafiq could not deny the love that he had developed for her when they were teens. They were only friends at the time, but he always wondered what things would be like if they were in a relationship together. Being sentenced to thirty-five years for a triple homicide that he did not commit made him lose hope of ever getting out of jail and having the life that he once dreamed of, but now that Boyce had given him hope, Rafiq was praying that everything went in his favor.

## 4

After spending the weekend stuck in the house with their son, Camilla was anxious to get out when Monday rolled around, but she wasn't looking forward to her weekly lunch date with her mother. Glancing at the clock on her nightstand, when she saw that it was five minutes until nine, Camilla rolled out of bed and headed down the hall to Kannon's room and noticed that he was already up and dressed for the day.

"Hey, baby boy," she greeted with a smile. "Who got you up and dressed this morning?"

"Daddy before he left." Kannon's eyes remained focused on the TV.

"Oh really? Do you know where your Daddy went?"

"I promised that I wouldn't tell you, mommy." He glanced up at her.

"Okay, baby," Camilla chuckled. "Well stay here until I'm done getting dressed, Kannon."

"Okay, mommy."

She gave her son a quick kiss before heading back down the

hall to her master bedroom to get washed. As Camilla handled her hygiene, she wondered what her husband was up to. She was always the one that got Kannon washed and dressed in the mornings because Kane had to go to work. So, for him to do this had her mind racing, but since their son knew what his father was up to, Camilla figured it couldn't be bad and put her mind at ease. Once she was finished in the bathroom, she got dressed in a pair of light denim Polo jeans and a white Polo blouse with a pair of Louis Vuitton monogram knee boots, then headed over to her vanity to fix her hair and do her make-up. When she was finished, Camilla stood in front of the full-length mirror checking herself out and she smiled at her beauty. Her 5'6" inch frame was one of perfection. Her light brown skin was blemish and pimple free. Her dark brown hair was long and natural, and her body was on point. Her 36D breast, thick hips and round ass was enough to stop any man in his tracks but her dazzling eyes had the power to hypnotize anyone. After fixing one of her curls, Camilla snatched up her tan Polo cardigan and Louis Vuitton monogram tote before she left her room. She helped Kannon with his jacket before taking him by the hand and guiding him outside to her black 2019 Lexus RX. After strapping her son in his seat, she jumped behind the wheel, revved the engine, and pulled off.

An hour later, Camilla arrived at her parents' five-bedroom, eight-bathroom mansion in Sandy Springs. Parking next to her mothers' car, she grabbed her purse, helped her son out of the car, and headed towards the backyard where Kannon took off running once he saw his grandmother.

"Hi, Grandma!" he shouted, wrapping his arms around her legs.

"Hello, my handsome grandson." Maggie smiled, leaning down to kiss him.

"Hey, mom." She kissed her mothers' cheek with a smile.

"What's wrong?" Maggie eyed her suspiciously.

"What? Where did that come from?" Camilla gasped.

"Camilla Ann Hayes-Jacobs, don't you lie to me." Her mother placed a hand on her hip.

Camilla's eyes shifted from Maggie to her son, who was staring at her.

"Kannon, baby, go play and I'll call you when it's time to eat."

"Okay."

Camilla waited until her son was out of earshot before talking.

"Mom, how do you always know when something is wrong with me?"

"Because I know my child. Now what's wrong?"

"I'm...I'm not happy with my life, mom," she answered honestly.

When her mother began to laugh, Camilla gazed at her as if she were crazy.

"Are you serious, child?"

"I'm dead ass serious, mom," she stated sternly.

"How could you not be happy with your life, Camilla? You're a young, beautiful and intelligent woman with a handsome, successful husband who thinks the world of you and he takes damn good care of you. You got money in your bank account. You drive a nice car and live in a beautiful mansion. What is there not to be happy about?" Maggie asked in confusion.

"I don't have a life of my own, mom. Everything you just said I have was provided for me because of Kane. If that nigga was to divorce my ass today or tomorrow, I wouldn't have shit to my name," Camilla expressed with frustration. "I had plans on going to college after I graduated high school and start a business of some sort. Not just be a housewife that shopped and stayed in the house all day. Like you said, I'm young, intelligent and beautiful. I should be doing more with my life."

"Do you hear yourself right now?" Maggie placed her hands on Camilla shoulders. "There are women out there who would kill to stay at home and shop all day instead of punching a clock or going to school. You have an easy care-free life, honey."

"Yeah. An easy care-free life that I was forced into." Camilla pulled out of her mother's grasp.

"What did you say?" Maggie asked in shock.

"I don't mean no disrespect mom, but I was persuaded into marrying Kane by you and Daddy. I wasn't ready to be a wife at the age of eighteen, but you and dad wouldn't let up until I said yes. Don't get me wrong. I love Kane. I really do but who he is now is not the man I fell in love with and every time I tell you about how he talks to me and treats me some time, you just tell me to deal with it and stop doing shit to make him treat me that way. You raised me to *never* let anyone disrespect or mistreat me, but then you tell me to tolerate it from my husband, which is confusing as hell," Camilla ranted.

"Now, look! I will not stand here and let you talk to me any kind of way in my own house, Camilla." Maggie pointed her finger at her. "And as far as being pressured into marrying Kane, you can call it whatever you want, but your father and I did your ass a favor. We saved you from going down the path of destruction and gave you a life that you woulda had to struggle to get on your own. The crowd you were hanging around wasn't good for you, which is why we moved here when you were sixteen. Those hood rats and thugs you were hanging with were going to get you into trouble and we had to save you from that life. So, instead of being an ungrateful brat, you need to be thankful for the life your parents and husband have provided for you. Now, let's go eat."

Camilla eyes burned with tears as she watched her mother walked away. She couldn't believe that her mother called her an ungrateful brat. Most mothers would have encouraged their children to do things that made them happy. Not deal with a life that wasn't satisfying to them. It was mind-boggling to Camilla as to why her mother would tell her to accept the life that was given to her instead of telling her to be all she could, like Maggie had been preaching to her all her life.

After a tension-filled lunch, Camilla allowed her son to hug and kiss his grandmother good-bye while she rolled her eyes at her mother before storming off to her car. As she strapped Kannon in his car seat, Camilla saw Maggie standing in the doorway looking at her. Closing the door, the women stared daggers at each other before Camilla hopped in her car and drove off. She was hoping that once she was out of her mother's presence that her anger would subside, but it didn't. The conversation she had with Maggie was on repeat in her head like a favorite song. Needing a pick me up, Camilla stopped at Kroger for some chocolate-chip cookie dough ice cream and some snacks for Kannon. While she was standing in the express checkout line, she saw a woman a couple of lanes over that looked familiar to her. She continued to stare at the woman trying to get a better look at her. When the woman looked in her direction, her eyes grew wide as if she knew who she was. As they stared at each other, a customer that was standing behind Camilla cleared his throat, letting her know that she could go. Quickly paying for her purchases, she grabbed her bags and Kannon's hand before leaving out of the store. Camilla debated with herself on whether or not she should wait for the girl to come out of the store or just leave. Deciding to leave, she stopped in her tracks when she heard her name being called.

"Camilla? Camilla Hayes?"

"Yes?" She turned around to see the woman that was calling her.

"It's me. Nakia Brown. Bitch don't act like you don't remember me."

"Oh my God! I knew you looked familiar!" Camilla shouted as the women embraced each other.

"Girl! You don't know how much I miss you." Nakia broke their embrace. "Me and my husband was just talking about you the other day."

"Your husband?"

"You remember Boyce, right?"

"Yeah. The guy you were dating when we were kids."

"Yeah. That's my husband." Nakia flashed a cheesy smile and her ring.

"Oh my God! I always knew y'all were gonna get married. You were crazy about his ass when we were kids," Camilla teased.

"And I'm even more crazy about his ass now, okay?" she seriously stated. "And who is this lil man?"

"This my son, Kannon. Kannon, this is my best friend, Nakia."

"Hello, handsome," she cooed.

"Hello, pretty lady." He smiled.

"Damn, Camilla. You got a flirt on your hands," Nakia chuckled, "Uh oh! And a ring on your finger too! Bitch, you married too?"

"Yup. I've been married for four years now."

"Girl this is just too much for me. I reunite with my best friend and she has a whole husband and baby. I need ya number. We got some serious catching up to do."

"Indeed."

The women exchanged numbers and hugs before going their separate ways. Once she got Kannon situated, Camilla pulled out of the parking lot with a smile on her face. Seeing her best friend again after seven long years made her forget about the conversation she had with Maggie. Nakia and

Camilla were thick as thieves when they were growing up. The two girls first cross paths at a neighborhood playground where Nakia teased and bullied her for the way she dressed and the clothes she wore. At the age of seven, Camilla was decked out in designer clothes while young Nakia had on non-name brand clothes and her hair was a mess. After Nakia had the whole playground calling her a conceited little rich girl, Camilla's feelings were hurt. She didn't fit in with the rest of the kids, but after Camilla beat Nakia's ass on the playground, all the kids were singing a different tune, and they started teasing Nakia. Camilla enjoyed being the popular kid at the playground, but when she saw how hurt and down Nakia was, she befriended her and they were inseparable until Camilla's parents moved her away and cut her off from Nakia.

When Camilla made it home, she and Kannon entered the house before she stopped in their tracks and stared at the sight before her. The large bouquets of roses along with shopping bags from her favorite stores, and 'I'm sorry' balloons were on the table in the hallway.

"Surprise, mommy!" Kannon giggled. "Do you like it?"

"I love it!" she beamed. "So this is what your daddy had planned huh?"

"Yeah. He wanted to do something nice for you to make up for being mean to you on Friday."

"Oh really," Camilla gasped.

"Mmm hmm."

Closing the door behind her, she walked over to the large bouquet of flowers, removing the card from the holder.

*I'm sorry for the way I treated you and I promise that you're gonna see a change in me Camilla. I love you and I don't wanna lose you*

In disbelief, she read the short message ten times more just to make sure she wasn't tripping. The last time Kane surprised her with gifts was when they were in the beginning stages of their relationship but what she was surprised about the most was that he actually apologized to her, even if it was written and not verbal, he still did, which was a first a first. The ringing of her phone interrupted the moment she was having. Camilla retrieved her phone from her purse and smiled harder when she saw it was Kane calling her.

"Hey, baby," she greeted. "I love my surprise."

"I'm glad you do, baby. I know it's been years since I've done something like this, but I wanted to do something different. I know the things I brought you won't make up for the way I treated you over the years, but I was hoping that this would be the start of us making up and starting over," Kane spoke sincerely.

"I would love that, Kane. What time will you be home, so we can start making up the right way," she asked in a seductive tone.

"I'll be home by seven, but...I'm gonna have to go outta town tomorrow to handle some business. Something came up at one of the offices were setting up in North Carolina, and I'm gonna be gone for two weeks."

Camilla instantly became pissed at the words Kane spoke because, once again, business was getting in the way of their quality time, but since they were on the path to starting over, she decided to take the high road and meet her husband halfway.

"No problem Kane. Would you like me to start getting your bag ready or do you wanna do it?"

"Uh...I... I'll do it, bae," he stammered.

"Okay, baby. I'll see you when you get home."

"O...Okay."

Ending the call, Camilla laughed at Kane's reaction to what she said. She felt good leaving her husband at a loss for words. After placing her melting ice cream in the freezer and put the snacks away, Camilla gathered the shopping bags and carried them upstairs to her room. Although her day started out bad, it ended up being a pretty good day for Camilla. With her and Kane starting over in their marriage and reconnecting with her best friend, she felt as though her unsatisfying life might become eventful after all.

# 5

"Yeesss, Daddy. Go deeper!" Camilla shouted.

"Not so loud, bae. You gonna wake up our son," Kane chuckled, nibbling on her ear.

"I'm sorry, but this shit feels so damn good," she moaned.

Keeping his medium speed, Kane obeyed his wife's command and pushed deep inside of her causing her to dig her nails into his back. He embraced the pain as he continued to drive his wife crazy. After fucking all night, he was surprised when Camilla woke him up with some head, and he couldn't refuse the urge had to dive back into his pussy one more time before he hit the road. The passionate, long kisses and the pounding he was delivering had Kane on brink of exploding and by the way his wife's legs were shaking, so was Camilla.

"Oh my God Kane! I'm about to cuumm!"

"So am I," he grunted.

Keeping the same pace, the couple climaxed minutes later riding out their high. Kane kissed Camilla's forehead before sliding out of her wetness. He smiled as he watched his wife curl into a ball and wrap herself up in the blankets. It had been a while since they had sex like that and by the way Camilla put it on his ass, Kane was ready to say fuck his trip and stay home, but he couldn't. Heading towards the bathroom, he ran the water for his shower and stepped inside. Once he was clean from head to toe, he washed his face, brushed his teeth, and tossed on his grey Polo sweat suit with his wheat-colored Timberland Boots. With his suitcase in hand, he kissed Camilla and Kannon good-bye then made his way out the door. Tossing his suitcase in the trunk of his 2019 black Yukon Denali, Kane hopped behind the wheel, brought the car to life and pulled off.

As he headed towards I-85, his phone began to vibrate in his pocket. Keeping his focus on the road, he answered his phone and sighed before answering the call.

"Nigga, where the fuck you at? You told me that you would be here before six, and it's already 6:15. What the fuck!" The female's voice boomed through the phone.

"Calm the fuck down Sheena," he roared. "I had to take care of some shit and it held me up! I'm on my way now! So, chill the fuck out aight!"

The phone fell silent for a moment before Sheena spoke again.

"I'm sorry for coming at you like that, Kane. I'm just scared right now. Our daughter has a temperature of 104.6 that won't break, and I wanted you to be here when I took her to the hospital," she stated calmly.

"Just take Kaylynn to the hospital, and I'll meet you there."

"Okay."

Ending the call, he placed the phone in the cup holder and turned up the volume letting, 2 Chains lyrics fill his car. As he drove down the expressway, Kane battled with himself about the lies he told over the years and the secrets that he had been keeping, and this was his greatest one. The affair that he had with Sheena was something that had been haunting him from the moment they fucked nearly two years ago. Kane had attended a business seminar in Savannah, and when he spotted Sheena from across the room, he was instantly drawn to her. They met each other for drinks that night and the rest was history. Although he wore a condom the night of his infidelity, the condom broke and Kane instantly regretted his action. When Sheena called four months later saying that she was pregnant, he wasn't surprised, but he still took a paternity test to be sure and Kane was indeed the father. Too embarrassed to let anyone know about his betrayal and outside baby, he kept Sheena and Kaylynn a secret. Even though the situation with Sheena was fling, he hated that he had to keep them a secret. She was, after all, the mother of his daughter, and his family had the right to know about them, but bringing them into the picture would destroy his marriage with the woman he loved and begged his father to be with. It would also break up his father's and Richard's twenty-five year friend/partnership, and Kane wasn't about to let that happen.

Three and a half hours later, Kane pulled in the emergency room parking lot of Memorial Health University Medical Center in Savannah, GA. Pulling into the nearest spot, he killed the engine and removed his wedding ring, placing it in the armrest of his truck. He snatched up his cell phone then headed inside the hospital taking a few breaths along the way. After telling the receptionist who he was there to see, the receptionist told Kane the room number his daughter was in. He thanked the male receptionist before heading to the back to find Sheena and Kaylynn. Knocking lightly on the door, he stepped into the room, and Kaylynn tried to break free from her mothers' arms, causing the doctor to stop mid-sentence.

"Doctor, this is Kaylynn's father." Sheena informed him.

"Nice to meet you, sir. I was just telling Miss Walters that Kaylynn has the flu. It could be caused by the weather changing or she could have caught it from another child at her daycare center. Since her flu is not causing her to have any difficulties with eating, drinking or urinating, I'm going to discharge her. I recommend that you give her children's Tylenol every four hours and plenty of fluids. Once you receive the discharge papers, you can take her home. If nothing changes, bring her back."

"Thank you, Doctor." Kane extended his hand to him.

"No problem." The doctor shook his hand giving a small smile before leaving.

"Please take this child before she jumps off my lap." Sheena handed him their daughter who gave him a big smile.

"Hey, daddy's baby," Kane cooed, "Daddy's baby got the flu huh? Don't worry about it 'cause I'm here now, and I'm gonna make you feel better," he smiled making her laugh.

"So because our daughter got the flu, you think I'm not doing a good job taking care of her?" she snapped.

"Sheena." Kane sighed. "I never said that. Kids get sick. So do adults, shit. Things happen. Kay having the flu is not your fault."

"Whatever, nigga." she rolled her eyes at him.

"What the fuck is your problem, Sheena? You've been tripping since you called me this morning." Kane glared at her.

"Nothing, just leave me alone." She dismissed him with a hand wave. "So how long are you here for?"

"A week."

"A week? That's longer than your usual three or four-day trips," Sheena stated with surprise.

"I know, but being as though I only come to visit once a month, I figured I can make the trip out here a lil longer. I be missing my baby girl." Kane smiled at Kaylynn who was falling asleep in his arms.

"That's all you miss?" She questioned with hope in her eyes.

"Yeah." He kept his eyes trained on his daughter.

The room fell silent as they waited for the doctor to return with the discharge papers. Kane felt a little bit bad for how he responded to Sheena's question, but he had to keep it real with her. Moments later, the doctor returned with the papers, explained everything once more and left. After he put Kaylynn's jacket on, they made their way out of the hospital and headed over to Sheena's car. Kane secured her in the car seat then closed the door.

"I'm gonna stop by a CVS or something and get Kay's medicine. Does she need anything else?" Kane asked.

"Can you get her a box of diapers size 2 and some milk?"

"No problem. I'll meet you at your crib in a minute."

"Okay."

Staring at each other for a moment, Kane noticed the seduction in Sheena's eyes, and he knew what she wanted. Instead of saying or doing anything, he walked away and hopped in his truck. Bringing his truck to life, Kane pulled off driving to the nearest CVS. Once he grabbed the items he needed, Kane parked in the driveway of Sheena's house. Meeting him at the door, Sheena moved to the side as he carried everything inside placing them on the dining room table. Kane removed the children's Tylenol from the bag and read the dosage before opening the box.

"Are you going to give that to her now?" Sheena asked in confusion.

"Yeah." He made his way over to Kaylynn's pack-n-play where she was sleeping. "Am I not supposed to?"

"I don't know if you should be giving her medicine while she's sleeping."

"That's the best time to give her medicine. That way, she doesn't try to fight you."

Placing the dropper in Kaylynn's mouth, Kane gently squeezed it and laughed at the face's their daughter made as she swallowed the nasty liquid.

"See." He smirked. "Piece of cake." He twisted the cap back on the bottle.

"Well I'll be damned." She shook her head. "For this to be your first baby, you sure are good at taking care of one."

"A few of my bruh's have kids, and I pay attention to them when their kids are in their care." He lied with no hesitation.

Kane headed to the kitchen to clean the dropper off and Sheena followed behind him.

"Kane?"

"Wassup?"

"What would you say if I told you that I wanted you to be around more?" She twiddled her thumbs.

"Say what?"

"This is our first child, and at times I feel like I don't know what I'm doing. I call my friends for advice and my parents come by to help me every weekend, but when they're gone, I'm all alone," Sheena expressed sadly. "I can't do this by myself, Kane. I need your help."

Kane stared at her for a moment to see if this was a con of some sort but by the expression displayed on her face, he could tell that Sheena was being sincere. Although he didn't know too much about her, he knew that Sheena was full of pride and independence. She wasn't the type to ask anyone for help unless she really needed it. Unable to ignore her plead, Kane needed to come up with a solution for their problem.

"I know it's not easy raising a child on your own. Especially the first one and I'm sorry I haven't been around as much to help you out with Kaylynn, but I promise I'm gonna work on that. I'm here for the week. So, let's try to make the most of this time and we'll come up with a solution before I leave. Aight?"

"Okay," she smiled, "I have to run some errands. Are you staying here or at a hotel?"

"I was gonna stay at a hotel but since Kaylynn sick, I think I'm gonna stay here so I can be around if you need me."

"Cool. I'll pick up something from the market on my home

for dinner." Sheena gathered her things and headed towards the door.

"Aight. See you when you get back."

When Sheena was out of sight, Kane made himself comfortable on the couch and turned on the sixty-inch smart TV. Settling for college basketball, he removed his phone from his pocket to check on Camilla but before he could call her, a call came through from his wife.

"Hey, bae. I was just about to call you." He answered.

"Well I beat you to it," she chuckled. "Did you make it to your destination?"

"Yeah I did. I stopped at the building first to check on things. I just got settled in my hotel room not too long ago." Kane lied through his teeth. "What you doing? How's Kannon?"

"We just got finished playing outside. This boy has way too much energy for me," Camilla laughed.

"He gets it from his father," Kane stated in a seductive tone."

"Shut up, Kane."

They laughed.

"So, what are y'all gonna do while I'm away?" He questioned.

"Besides missing you, I'm gonna link up with an old girl-friend of mines that I ran into yesterday while I was at the market."

"Old girlfriend? I didn't know you had friends at all." Kane leaned forward on the couch.

"I had lots of friends before I met you, Kane. My parents cut me off from all of my friends by moving me to Sandy Springs when I was sixteen but seeing my best friend Nakia again after all these years brought back a lot of old memories and fun times." He could tell his wife was smiling by her tone.

"Are you going to visit her at her house or she is coming over there?"

"Does it matter, Kane?"

"Yes, it does," he raised his voice while jumping to his feet. "One, I don't want just anyone in my house and two, I don't want you and my son traveling to an unfamiliar location."

"You don't want just anyone in your house?" Camilla scoffed. "I thought that this was my house too, Kane?"

"It is Camilla. You know I didn't mean it like that." He tried to correct himself.

"Then what did you mean?"

"I'm just saying. You haven't seen this girl in years. She might be trying to set you up or something," Kane panicked.

"Wow," she gasped in disbelief. "So much for starting over huh?"

"What you mean?"

"Throughout our entire marriage, I've done everything you wanted me to do. I never go anywhere besides the normal places and I don't interact with anyone but you and the family and the first time I say I'm gonna link up with my friend, you're trying to find a way to shut me down like you always do," she angrily expressed.

"I'm not tryna shut you down Camilla. I'm just thinking about y'all safety," he explained.

"No! You're trying to control what I do and who I talk to!"

Caught off guard by her words, Kane was at a loss for words and didn't know how to respond.

"Baby, I know this is something new because you've never known me to have people in my life outside of the family but if you trust me like I trust you, this shouldn't be a problem, Kane," Camilla softly spoke.

"You trust me for real?"

"Of course, I do, baby. You've never given me a reason not to," she answered honestly. "Do you trust me?"

"No doubt," Kane responded with confidence.

"Then please be open to this, bae," she begged. "How about

this. When you come back, I can introduce you to Nakia and her husband. Does that sound like a plan?"

"Yes, it does, Camilla," he nervously answered.

"Thank you, Daddy," she replied cheerfully. "I love you so much."

"I love you too, bae. I'm gonna call you a lil bit later. I'm about to chill for a minute and watch some basketball.

"Okay. Talk to you later."

Ending the call, Kane tossed his phone on the table and began pacing the floor. Even though he agreed to let Camilla spend time with her friend and for him to meet them when he returned home, Kane was dead set against it. He wasn't used to his wife having friends and now that she reunited with her best friend, he feared the changes that might come with her having a social life but since they were supposed to be starting over, Kane decided to ease up and see how things turned out. He trusted his wife to the fullest and knew that she wouldn't betray him but knowing that Camilla trusted him the same way as he did her caused his heart to break. The fact that Kane just had a whole conversation with his wife in his baby mama's house only made things worse on his end. After pondering on the situation some more, he wasn't sure if he agreed because of the trust he had in his wife or the guilt from his own betrayal. Whichever one it was, Kane was going to have to find a way to handle the changes that were coming.

## 6

A s Nakia cleaned her house from top to bottom, excitement flowed through her body as she prepared to see Camilla again. Words could not express how much she missed her best friend. Going years without being with her bestie drove her crazy and although Nakia had friends at her job and in her book club, none of them measured up to Camilla and the special bond they shared. Since bumping into her at the market a few days prior, all she did was think about the times they shared together and how they always had each other's backs. Camilla was more like a sister to her than a friend and when her parents ended their friendship, it shattered Nakia's world.

After she finished cleaning the entire house, she went into the kitchen and began preparing dinner. Fried chicken, collard greens, Rice-a-Roni, and cornbread was on the menu, and her homemade sweet potato pie was for dessert. Nakia decided to cook all of her besties favorite foods to show her that she did not forget about her. As she maneuvered around the kitchen, Nakia heard the keys jingling and knew her husband and the kids were home from their weekly outing.

"Mommy!" Her four-year-old son, Boyce Junior, shouted running into the kitchen.

"Hey, baby!" she smiled scooping him up into her arms. "Did you have fun today?"

"Yes. Daddy took me and Breyanna to the Coca-Cola Center, and he bought us a bunch of things from the gift shop."

"He did?"

"I sure did." Boyce entered the kitchen with their two-year old daughter in his arms. "BJ picked out like three things but this lil one here wanted everything she picked up," he smiled at his daughter.

"That doesn't surprise me. She does the same thing to me whenever we go to Walmart," Nakia chuckled before kissing her husband's lips.

Boyce shook his head as he helped Breyanna out of her jacket and placing her on the floor.

"Mommy, is you friend and her son still coming over?

"They sure are," Nakia grinned. "Camilla called me this morning and said she'll be her by six." She placed BJ on his feet

"Is her son cool like me?"

"He seemed like he was one of the cool kids," she laughed, "He's handsome and a lady's man like you are." Nakia gently pinched his cheeks.

"I might like this kid. What's his name?"

"His name is Kannon."

"Kannon? With a name like that, he gotta be cool."

BJ's comment made both of his parents laugh.

"Take your sister to your playroom and go play for a while," Boyce spoke, "We'll let you know when he gets here."

"Okay Daddy."

They watched as BJ took Breyanna by the hand and walked her down the hall.

"That boy is definitely your son, bae."

"Who you telling," he shook his head. "Damn Kia. You got it

smelling good in here. You need to invite Camilla over more often. It's been a while since you threw down like this."

"Shut up. Boyce." She laughed. "I know I don't cook like this all the time but after spending hours baking at the bakery, the last thing I wanna do is come home and cook but when I do, I make enough food to last us for the week. So, don't be acting like I don't cook for ya ass."

"I'm just fucking with you, bae." He held his up in surrender. "I can't believe Camilla is married with a kid. Did she tell you who her husband is?"

"Nah, but by the rock and wedding band that she was rocking, I know she ain't married to no hood nigga or drug dealer, and knowing her boujie ass parents, they probably fixed Camilla up with one of their rich friend's sons."

"You think so?"

"I know so." She glanced up at him. "They ran every inch of her life. They didn't like her hanging out with me because my parents weren't as wealthy as they were. I could never go over to Camilla's house because they thought I was gonna steal something from her, but my mom welcomed Camilla with open arms despite the things her parents said about me. She didn't act stuck up like her parents and that's what my mom loved about her and I was the only friend that didn't ask her for money or tried to leech off of her," Nakia ranted," So yeah. I'm pretty sure she's married to some rich nigga."

"Damn. I didn't know her parents were that bad. Now I see why she had to sneak to do everything," Boyce stated in shock. "I'm happy that she's married, but this is kinda upsetting news."

"Why you say that?"

"Because I think Rafiq still has feelings for Camilla, and when I tell him this, this is going to fuck him up."

"You mean to tell me that Rafiq still has a thing for Camilla after all these years?" Nakia gasped.

"Hell yeah. When I told him you saw her at the market, he

was happier than a motherfucker and now that everything is going well with his case, he might be getting out in the next couple of months or so. The only thing is Rafiq was hoping to hook up with Camilla," Boyce added.

"Awww," she pouted, "Well just because they're married doesn't mean they can't be friends." She shrugged.

"Do you know how difficult it is to just be friends with someone you're in love with and you gotta watch them be happy with someone else? That shit ain't easy to do, bae."

"You're right about that." Nakia nodded her head. "Let's not think about that right now and don't mention Rafiq to Camilla. Aight?"

"Aight. I'ma go chill in the bedroom. Let me know when they get here." Boyce kissed her cheek before heading upstairs.

Learning that Rafiq still had a thing for her bestie after all these years brought a smile to her face. She thought it was cute how he still held Camilla in his heart even though he had not seen her in years. She remembered how they always tried to deny how much they liked each but even a blind person could see how crazy in love they were when they were teenagers. Rafiq, as well as Camilla, would get mad if another girl or boy was in each other's face. They tried to keep things between them on a friendship level, but it was hard for them to control their feelings for one another.

Once Nakia was finished with dinner, she placed everything on the dining room table and covered it to keep the food warm. Placing the last dish on the table, she went to freshen up and changed out of her cami and yoga pants into a pair of navy-blue Nike sweatpants, white Nike tank top and white ankle socks. As she finished putting her black twenty-inch Remy hair into a bun, the doorbell sounded throughout the house. Scurrying to the front door with her husband in tow, Nakia took a deep breath before opening it.

"Hey, Kia," Camilla sang with Kannon in her arms.

"Hey, C!" She threw her arms around them hugging them tightly.

"Wassup, Camilla?" Boyce smiled at her.

"Wassup, Boyce!" Camilla made her way inside the house and gave him a quick hug. "You still tryna take over the world?"

"And you know this," he responded, causing them to laugh. "And you must be Kannon. Nice to meet you, sir." He put his fist out for a pound.

Kannon dapped him up finishing with a fist bump and Boyce nodded his head.

"Yeah. You're definitely one of the cool kids," he chuckled.

"Oh goodness!" Camilla gasped at the sight of their children. "And who are these lil ones?" She placed Kannon on his feet.

"Camilla, this is our son BJ and our daughter Breyanna. Kids, this is mommy's best friend, Camilla and her son Kannon."

"It's nice to meet y'all," Camilla smiled at them.

"Nice to meet you too, pretty lady," BJ flirted.

"Wow!" she gasped.

"I told you I had one of my own," Nakia laughed. "Come on y'all so we can eat. I made all of your favorites, girl."

"I smell the fried chicken in the air," Camilla stated as they headed to the dining room. "I bet you made it the same way your mom used to make it when we were kids."

"Yup. Check it out." She removed the lid exposing the chicken.

"Mmm hmmm." Camilla nodded her head as she watched her bestie remove all of the lids from the containers. "Everything looks delicious."

"And it tastes even better than it looks," Boyce chimed in, taking a seat at the table.

The ladies helped the kids get seated before taking their own seats. Joining hands, Boyce blessed the food before they began fixing their plates. As Camilla bit into her chicken, Nakia watched and waited for her reaction. Seeing the look of pleasure displayed on her besties face warmed her heart.

"Oh my God, Kia! This chicken tastes exactly like your moms," she raved.

"I'm glad you like it." Nakia grinned.

"I see you didn't forget much about me over the years."

"You damn right I didn't."

As they continued to chow down, Nakia spent most of her time asking questions instead of eating. She wanted to know about all of the exciting things Camilla had been up to over the years but when she learned that her bestie was just a housewife who spent most of her days shopping, working out and having weekly lunch with her mother, Nakia was a little disappointed. Although Camilla was unsure about what her future held, the one thing Nakia remembered her saying was that she wanted to attend an HBCU, join a sorority and obtain a degree. She didn't understand for the life of her why her friend wasn't doing more with her life but after listening to Camilla explain what type of man her husband was, everything became clear to Nakia. Her best friend was married to a controlling asshole who wanted to keep Camilla sheltered and hidden from the world, just like her parents did. The disappointing news about Camilla's life caused Nakia to lose her appetite and she shut down for the rest of the night.

Instead of spending the rest of the evening going through her photo album like she had planned, Nakia ended the night early by telling Camilla that she wasn't feeling well and needed to lay down. She had a feeling that Camilla knew she was lying but instead of her best friend protesting, they exchanged hugs and promised to stay in touch. As soon as Camilla and Kannon were gone, Nakia vented to her husband.

"What the fuck I tell you, Boyce? I told you her parents fixed her up with some rich asshole but the fact that she's married to someone as controlling as her parents is what pisses me off the most! she shouted.

"Baby. Just calm down." he placed his hands on her shoulders. "I know that you're upset about Camilla and the life she is living but it's her life Nakia and from the outside looking in, she seems happy."

"I know she *seems* happy, but I don't know if she really is," she sighed, "I just knew that Camilla had went to college, got her degree and was either working or running her own business or something. Not just keeping in shape for her man and making sure she looked good for him while taking care of their son. We've had countless conversations about what we wanted to do when we got older and this wasn't in the plan. What happened to her?"

"When you're young, naive and easy to persuade, it's very easy for people to manipulate and take advantage of you. Especially if you don't have a mind of your own," Boyce explained.

Nakia nodded her head in understanding.

"Well I gotta do something. I just can't stand by and let my friend waste her life." She walked back to the dining room and began placing the lids on the containers.

"I know you feel like you need to save her, but you can't do that. Y'all just came back into each other's lives, and if you tell Camilla she's not living hers right, she's gonna distance herself from you," he stated sternly. "Instead of trying to save her, encourage her to get out more. You're involved in a book club, and you're a part of a mentoring program for young girls. You have your own business. You have a life outside of me and the kids. Show Camilla that. Invite her to your book club meeting so she can meet some people. Help her find her life, Nakia."

Letting her husband's words sink in, she realized that Boyce was on to something. Although Nakia wanted to tell Camilla that she was in a controlling relationship and needed to break free, she decided to follow her man's advice and show her that it was more to life than being a housewife and by her doing so, she hoped that it would encourage her friend to live her life to the fullest.

# 7

The sound of Camilla's phone ringing caused her to steer in her sleep. She knew it was Kane calling by the ringtone and snatched her phone off the nightstand.

"Good morning baby," she sleepily greeted when the FaceTime call connected.

"Hey, baby. How was the dinner with your friends last night?"

"It was fun," she smiled. "I enjoyed seeing them again and the food was so good! We had fried chicken, greens, cornbread—"

"You ate all that fattening shit," He frowned. "You're gonna have to put in double the work the next time you work out."

"Really, Kane?"

"I'm just saying."

"Anyway, how is your trip going?" she asked dryly.

"It's going good. I'm actually on my way to Philly for a business meeting and if things go right, our software might be used in a couple of major companies up there."

"That's great, Kane. I guess the expansion project is going well?"

"Yes, it is and because it's going well, I want us to celebrate with a trip."

"A trip? You're really gonna take me on a trip? Camilla sat up in the bed.

"Yup. Just me and you. I'll let you pick the place." He smiled.

"Okay, baby." She returned the smile.

"You look into that and I'll call you when I touch down in Philly. I love you."

"I love you too, Kane."

Ending the call, Camilla sat in deep thought for a moment replaying the conversation with her husband. The fact that he didn't acknowledge the good time she had with Nakia and Boyce bothered her a little but what bothered her the most was that he cared about what she ate and how she was going to have to work that fattening food off more. The meal that Nakia prepared for her was the most filling meal Camilla had eaten in a while. Although she ate healthy food most of the time, she always felt hungry throughout the day and last night, she didn't go to bed starving. Kane had never said no shit like that to her before, and it made her wonder if he was really in love with her or the way she looked. Camilla wanted to believe that her looks wasn't the only thing that Kane loved about her and the fact that she couldn't convince herself otherwise caused her to wonder.

The sound of her phone ringing interrupted her thoughts. Not really in the mood to talk, Camilla still checked her phone to see who was calling her. When she saw it was Nakia calling, she quickly answered.

"Hey, Kia. How are you feeling?"

"Huh? Oh, I feel better. It was just a lil upset stomach."

"Okay." She chuckled, "So wassup?"

"Do you remember those hood books I used to read when we were younger?"

"You mean the books your mama called smut books?" Camilla laughed.

"Yeah," she laughed as well, "I still read those types of books. I actually started a book club and I wanted to invite you to a meeting."

"A book club meeting?"

"Yeah. We pick different books from urban fiction authors, read them and share our thoughts on them at the meeting. We have little refreshments, talk and chill. It's really fun, C."

"I don't know Kia. I've never been that big on reading and my husband might not approve of me going to unfamiliar places and being around strangers."

"Aww come on Camilla. Don't let that nig—I mean, okay but if you change your mind, we meet at my house every Wednesday at 7:30 p.m. I'll send you the link to the book were reading. Just in case you change your mind."

"Okay. That's cool."

"Please think about coming, C."

"I will, Nakia. I'll talk to you later."

Placing her phone back on the nightstand, Camilla tossed the covers off of her and hopped out of bed. She was on her way to the bathroom when her doorbell rang.

"I just can't catch a break this morning." She sighed.

Putting on her robe, Camilla walked down the hall and Kannon rushed out of his room beating her to the door. She looked through the peephole and when she saw her father in law on the other side, she answered.

"Grandpa!" Kannon shouted causing Camilla to smile.

"Wassup, lil man?" Karl scooped his grandson up in his arms.

"Good morning, Karl." She kissed his cheek before letting him in. "How are you doing this morning?"

"I'm great," he confidently answered, "I just came over to see y'all and chat with my son for a minute."

"You know that we're always happy to see you, but Kane isn't here. He's been gone since last week." Camilla folded her arms across her chest.

"A week?" He asked in confusion. "Where did he go?"

"He went to North Carolina because there was a problem with the building that's being built over there and now he's on his way to Philly for a business meeting."

Noticing the change in Karl's mood caused Camilla to become suspicious.

"Is everything okay, Karl?"

"Yeah. I'm just a little upset that Kane wouldn't let me know about the moves he's making," he replied calmly.

"He didn't tell you that he was gonna be gone for two weeks on business?"

"Two weeks huh?" he chuckled, "You know what? I do recall him mentioning something about that. It must be this old age catching up to me." He smiled, easing the tension. "Well let me get on outta here and head over to the office for a minute. I'll see y'all later."

"Okay."

Camilla hugged her father-in-law good-bye before closing the door and locking it.

The brief encounter with Karl caused her mind to race as she made her way to the kitchen. From what she knew about him, he had the memory of an elephant and didn't forget anything. So, for him to pretend like he forgot that his son told him about his trip was some bullshit. Camilla wasn't sure who it was but one of them were lying about something and she hoped it wasn't Kane.

After making breakfast for her and Kannon, Camilla got him washed and dressed before she began cleaning their rooms. Pushing her thoughts about Kane and if he was lying about his whereabouts to the back of her mind, she thought back to the conversation she had with Nakia earlier that day and what she was about to say before she cut herself off. If memory served her correctly, Nakia was never the type to hold her tongue. She spoke her mind to anybody and didn't give a fuck about how they felt afterwards. So, for her to cut herself off in mid-sentence made her curious about what she really wanted to say.

By the time she finished cleaning up, Camilla had given herself a migraine from thinking so much and needed a way to escape her thoughts. Not in the mood to shop or workout, she thought about the book Nakia wanted her to checkout. She snatched her phone up off the nightstand, went to the messages and hit the link to the book. The title of the book was Thug Holiday and when she saw that the book had four authors, Camilla instantly thought that the book wasn't going to be well written but once she read the synopsis, she was intrigued. She paid the small fee for kindle unlimited and downloaded the book. Camilla called Kannon to her room, so she could keep an eye on him and began to read. From the first page of the book, she was hooked, and she instantly got wrapped up in the lives of the Holiday sisters.

When a call from Kane came through on her phone, Camilla was about to decline it so she could go back to reading but she answered it anyway.

"Hey, bae," she greeted with a smile.

"Who the fuck told you to tell my dad that I was outta town for two weeks!"

"I didn't know it was supposed to be a secret, Kane. Being as though you're on a business trip, I thought you woulda told your dad about it," Camilla shot back. "And being as though you're this mad that I told him, that must mean you did something wrong. So, what happened?"

"I don't wanna talk about it," he sighed. "I fucked up and

now I gotta fix it. I'm sorry for snapping on you like that. I couldn't snap on my dad, so I took my frustrations out on you and you didn't deserve that," Kane calmly apologized. "My dad cut my trip short. So, I'll be home a couple of days early."

"Okay, baby. I can't wait to see you," she cooed.

"I can't wait to see you either, baby. Let me get some sleep and I'll talk to you in the morning."

"Okay, Kane."

Ending the call, she noticed that it was close to eight at night and was blown away that she spent most of the evening reading. Deciding to take a break from the book she was so engrossed in, Camilla spent some time with Kannon before making him something to eat and putting him to bed. When her baby boy was sound asleep, Camilla got comfortable underneath her covers, and ended her night reading the rest of Thug Holiday. That was her first time reading any type of book since she graduated high school, and now that Camilla was introduced to the world of urban fiction, she added reading to her list of hobbies.

fter a successful business meeting in Philly, Kane was feeling like he was that nigga because he sealed the deal without the help of his father or Richard but every time he tried to think about the positive, the fact that he still had to face Karl when he returned home put him in a negative space. Even though he apologized to Camilla a few days before for opening her mouth, he still wanted to choke the hell out of her but after analyzing the situation some more, Kane realized she didn't have a choice but to tell her dad about his trip because he popped up at their house unannounced. So, he was right to apologize because he had no one to blame but himself.

When his flight touched down in Savannah, Kane hopped in an Uber and headed over to Sheena's house to pick up his truck. Being as though it was Wednesday, he knew that she was at work and since Kaylynn no longer had the flu, she was in daycare. He wanted to convince Sheena to take the day off so he could spend a couple of hours with his daughter before he returned to Atlanta, but Kane knew she wouldn't go for that. Pulling up to Sheena's house, Kane was surprised to see

Kaylynn sitting on the lap of an older gentleman that he assumed was her grandfather.

"Aww shit," he mumbled under his breath.

He hopped out the Uber and removed his luggage from the trunk before making his way to the front porch where they were sitting.

"You must be Kane." The older gentleman stood to his feet.

"Yes, sir. Kane Jacobs." He extended his hand to him.

"Thomas Walters. Pleasure to meet you son." He shook Kane's hand. "I apologize if you feel like you were caught off guard by my presence but when Sheena told me that you would be here to pick up your truck, I just had to meet you. You understand why, don't you?"

"Yes, sir. You wanted to meet the father of your grand-daughter and to see what type of man I was," Kane replied.

"Exactly," he chuckled. "When Sheena told me and her mother about her situation, I assumed you were some slick talking thug with no job and no manners but talking to you and seeing you in person, I see you are quite the opposite, which is a relief to me." Thomas handed Kaylynn over to him. "I understand that you were here for a week when Kaylynn had the flu."

"Yes, sir. I don't get to spend time with her that much and since she was sick, I decided to be here to help Sheena with our child," he answered honestly.

"And you being here meant a lot to my daughter," Thomas added. "I don't mean to overstep my bounds by asking this, but why aren't you and Sheena in a relationship? I don't see a ring on your finger, so I know you're not married."

"Sheena and I are not together simply because I'm not ready," he lied. "I have thought about us being together on a few occasions, but it would be selfish of me to get into a relationship with her knowing that I can't be there for her the way she needs me to be, and I didn't want her to uproot her life or vice versa for us to be together as well."

"Wow," Thomas gasped. "Most young men would string women along until they got things figured out but it's nice to know that you're considerate of my daughter's feelings."

Kane smiled and nodded.

"As much as I'm enjoying this time with y'all, I'm afraid I have to hit the road." He kissed his daughter's cheek before Thomas took her from his arms.

"I understand, son. I'm glad you took the time to talk to me."

"No problem, sir. It was a pleasure," Kane smiled.

Shaking hands, he kissed his baby girl once more before tossing his luggage in the trunk and hopping behind the wheel. Bringing the truck to life, he backed out of the driveway and when he saw Kaylynn crying for him, that shit broke his heart as he drove away. Kane hated himself for lying to Sheena's father, but he couldn't tell him the truth. It was bad enough that they had a one nightstand but having a one nightstand with a married man with a family was much worse. Feeling like shit, he drove to Atlanta in deep thought and mentally prepared himself to face his father.

Arriving nearly four hours later, Kane pulled into the driveway of his father's mansion and parked next to his father's car. He reached in the armrest for his ring and placed it back on his finger before he jumped out of his truck and made his way to the front door where his father buzzed him in. Kane closed the door behind himself then made his way to his father's office. He stood in the doorway until Karl motioned for him to come in. Pouring himself a drink, he took a seat in one of the office chairs, took a swig from his glass and waited for his father to finish his call.

"Aye, calm down. I understand that you're upset about this situation and I wish I could do more to help you out, but I can't. Somebody didn't do their part on your end to make this shit stick. So instead of breathing fire up my ass, direct that shit to your own people," Karl slammed the office phone down.

"Damn. That didn't sound like a business call," Kane calmly spoke.

"No, it wasn't, but don't worry about that," Karl sighed. "Now, do you care to explain to me why you lied to your wife about being in North Carolina for a week?"

"To be honest, dad, not really."

"Excuse me?" He glared at his son.

"You heard me right." Kane leaned forward in his chair. "What I do in my down time is my business and I shouldn't have to explain that to anybody," he stated angrily.

"When you go outta town and lie to your wife about your whereabouts that's a damn problem Kane," Karl roared. "If I woulda known you were outta town, I wouldn't have popped up at your house. I don't know what the fuck you got going on, son, but whatever it is, I hope that it doesn't jeopardize your marriage."

Kane glared at his father for a moment before responding.

"Dad, I understand what you had to go through in order to make my marriage happen with Camilla and I appreciate that, but my marriage is *my* business. You were against me getting married from the start and all you've done is tell me what to do without explaining shit to me. I made it this far on my own. So, let me continue to handle shit my way. Everything business related, I have no choice but to discuss it with you because you're my boss but everything else is none of your concern."

"You know what? Your right, Kane. I haven't been very supportive of your union and although I was against it, I shoulda done everything in my power to make it a success but being as though your ass is hard-headed, I knew you probably weren't gonna listen to my advice anyway. So, I'll stay outta your personal life, but I will tell you this, if you don't start doing right by that girl, some other man is gonna run off with wife," Karl warned.

Taking the rest of his drink to the head, Kane placed his glass on the desk and left the house without saying a word. Climbing in his truck, he put on T. I's 'Dime Trap' album then pulled out of the driveway and headed to Lenox mall to pick up a few things for his wife and son. After spending a couple of hours at the mall, Kane left with more shopping bags than he could carry. He couldn't wait to see the smile on Camilla's face when she saw the new clothes, shoes and handbags he bought her. Filling his trunk with the bags, Kane drove home ready to see his wife and son but when he saw that Camilla's car was gone, he stopped himself from becoming angry. He removed his phone the cupholder, called his wife and waited for her to answer.

"Hey, baby," she politely greeted.

"Don't *hey baby* me. Where the fuck are you with my son?"

"Kane, I sent you a text telling you that I was going to my friend's house for a book club meeting she's having and that I'll be home by ten," she explained.

"Book club meeting? When the fuck did you start reading?"

"A few days ago. I needed something to do with you being gone. So, my friend suggested that I join her club. I read the book, fell in love with it, and here I am. We'll be home when it's over, Kane."

"Nah the fuck you won't, Camilla! Bring ya ass home now!"

When the phone beeped indicating that the call ended, Kane let out a scream of frustration. He called her ten times back to back, but Camilla ignored his calls. Becoming furious, he went to the 'Find My Phone' app and tried to locate her, and when he discovered that she turned off her location, Kane banged his hands on the steering wheel. With his phone in hand, he stormed into the house and called his father-in-law.

He paced the floor to calm himself down some as he waited for him to answer.

"Hello, son. How's everything going?" Richard answered on the third ring.

"Everything is good, sir." He faked a smile. "I was calling to ask you if Camilla told you anything about reuniting with an old friend."

"No. She didn't, and I doubt if Maggie knows because they haven't talked to each other in about a week," he stated. "Is Camilla in some type of trouble?"

"Not at all. I just got back in town from being in Philly and I was excited about seeing her and my son but they weren't here. I called and told her to come home but she hung up on me," Kane played victim.

"I know my daughter, Kane, and she wouldn't just hang up on you for no reason," he chuckled. "Now did you ask her, or did you demand her to come home?"

"I demanded her too, sir," he grunted.

"Now I see why she hung up on you. You can't demand her to come home just because you want to see her and Kannon. I understand you miss her, but you should be happy that Camilla reunited with a friend and she's getting out of the house. I know that this is something that you're not used to, but you should at least see what happens before you try to shut my daughter down," Richard scolded.

"Excuse me, sir?"

"Maggie told me about the way that you've been disrespecting my daughter and trying to control the things she does and where she goes. When my wife told me this, I got upset with her because she thinks Camilla should deal with that shit but that's not how we raised her to be. I don't know what's going on with you Kane but my daughter is your wife and not a damn prisoner and whatever she wants to do, whether it's hang with her friends, go to school or whatever, you better give her the freedom to do so because if you don't start doing right by my daughter, I'll do everything in my power to make sure she divorces your ass and take everything you own. Do I make myself clear?"

"Yes, sir," Kane answered through gritted teeth.

"Good."

When Richard hung up on him, Kane was on the verge of exploding. He couldn't believe that Camilla told her mother about what was going on between them. Although he knew he was wrong for the way he treated Camilla, he didn't want anyone reading him his rights and telling him how he should treat his wife. Kane had just told his dad to stay out of his marriage, but he could not tell his in-laws to do the same because they were not his parents. Feeling defeated, there was nothing else for Kane to do but sit and wait for his wife and son to come home.

When the ten o'clock hour approached, he paced the floor waiting for them to come home. Once Kane calmed down, he thought about Camilla and the possibility of her not returning home. He told himself that he needed to work on his temper and to try to be more understanding, but he did not know how. Kane was used to his wife being home when he got home from work or returned from his business trips but now that Camilla was trying to have a life outside of him, he did not know how to handle it. Seeing the headlights of Camilla's car, Kane rushed to the door and opened it. He stood in the doorway until he saw her carrying a sleeping Kannon on her shoulder. As she walked by him, Kane locked the door behind them and followed behind Camilla. He watched as his wife undressed their son, put on his pajamas and tucked him in. After she kissed his forehead, his wife brushed past him without saying a word which meant that she was pissed with him.

"So, your just gonna walk passed me and not speak," he asked following behind her.

Camilla didn't respond.

"Whatever is on you mind Camilla, you need to speak on it because I'm not letting you go to sleep until you do."

"Fine." she quickly turned around to face him. "I'm tired of your controlling and demanding ass, Kane. You told me that you were gonna change and do better, but you've given little to no effort on you part. I know that you're not used to me having a life outside of this house besides shopping, but that shit is gonna change. So, your ass better roll with it or get rolled the fuck over because I'm tired of living and feeling like a prisoner," she angrily expressed, "And I already went ahead and enrolled Kannon into summer camp. It's time for him to start being around kids his own age and in September, he's starting pre-school." Camilla strolled into the closet.

"And where is this summer camp located at?" He followed her into the closet.

"In Marietta. My best friends' son goes there and since him and Kannon get along so well, I decided to send our son there. Is that a problem?" She placed her hands on her hips.

"Nah. That's cool. I feel the same way about Kannon being around kids his own age," Kane halfheartedly answered, "You know we coulda talked about this instead of you telling it to me like this."

"Kane, please. As soon as I woulda mentioned the topic of Kannon going to summer camp or school, you woulda shut me down like you always do without letting me explain because you want to keep me cooped up in this house," she brushed past him walking into the bedroom.

"Camilla." He gently grabbed her from behind. "I know I have anger issues and I'm not handling these changes so well. Every time you leave the house, I'm worried that something is gonna happen to you or that you're gonna leave me for someone else because of how I treat you."

"Those are your own insecurities that you have to deal with,

Kane." She stepped closer to him. "If you were doing right by me, you wouldn't feel this way and even though I hate the way you treat me sometimes, I never once thought about leaving you but if you keep this up and nothing changes, I'm not gonna have a choice because I will not tolerate this shit any longer," Camilla sternly stated.

"I'm sorry, baby."

Sealing his apology with a kiss, Kane picked Camilla up carrying her over to the bed where he laid her on her back. He pulled her to the edge of the bed, and dove headfirst into her pussy, eating her until he was tired. The conversation that they had opened his eyes to how serious his wife was about his intolerable behavior. If Camilla was determined to live her life, Kane wasn't going to stop her. He was just going to have to find another way to keep tabs on her to make sure she was being the loving, loyal and dedicated woman he married.

# 9

*Two Months Later...*

After spending six years, three months, and eight days as a prisoner in the Fulton County Jail, Rafiq Sanders was finally a free man. His patients were wearing thin with the long, tedious check out process but once that shit was over, he strolled out of the prison doors with his belongings in his hand stepping into the June summer heat. Scanning the parking lot, Rafiq didn't see his cousin nowhere. He was about to get in feelings because he told Boyce the day before to be there early but when he saw the money green 2019 Lincoln Navigator pull into the lot on twenty-four inch rims, Rafiq jogged over to the truck and admired it.

"God damn boy! This bitch cleaner than a motherfucker!" He nodded his head.

"Thanks, man," Boyce humbly grinned. "Get ya ass in here and let's get some grub my nigga."

"Say no more."

Rafiq excitedly jumped in the passenger seat, slammed the door shut and Boyce pulled out of the parking lot with screeching tires.

"So how does it feel to be a free man." Boyce turned the radio down.

"Honestly, I feel like I'm a new man," he grinned. "I thought I was gonna be behind bars for the rest of my life for something that I didn't do but now that I have a second chance at this shit, I'm gonna do shit right this time. Thanks again man for everything you did to get out me out. I'll spend the rest of my life paying you back cuz," Rafiq truthfully stated.

"You don't have to pay me back bro. I was just finishing the work that mom started. By you doing something positive with ya life, that will be payment enough for me and my mom." He glanced at his cousin. "My mom made sure that all of her kids would be straight when she passed on which means she left something for all of us. Including you. I'll give it to you when we get to the house."

"What is it?"

"Believe me when I tell you, it's something that you're gonna need to start ya new life," Boyce smiled.

"If you say so," he chuckled. "Aye, man. You never gave me an update on shawty."

"What, shawty?" he played dumb.

"Camilla, nigga."

"I know who you're talking about, man," he sighed. "Well Nakia ran into her at the market a couple of months back, and we've been spending most of our time getting to know her again."

"Okay. What else?"

"Camilla is... married... with a son, my nigga. I didn't want to tell you about her because I know you still have feelings for shawty," Boyce solemnly replied.

Learning that Camilla was married with a kid made his heart ache a little. Although Rafiq prayed that she remained unattached over the years, a part of him knew that she was probably tied down to somebody.

"Married with a kid huh?" He shook his head. "So, what is she doing with her life?"

"To be honest, Camilla didn't have a life until she reconnected with Kia. The only thing she used to do was exercise, shop and be a housewife. She ended up marrying a controlling asshole like her parents," Boyce stated, "Kia told me that her nigga be tripping on her because she has a life outside of him now but now that they've been hanging together for a few months, I guess that nigga chilled out which is strange to me."

"Why is that, cuz?" Rafiq questioned.

"Because as controlling as Camilla claims he is, ain't no way a nigga just gonna toss that shit aside overnight. I could be wrong but I got a feeling that nigga is keeping tabs on her some type of way and the reason he's been so cool is because he knows her every move"

"You think that nigga on some stalker type shit?"

"That nigga is big wig that's always outta town on business and lives at his office so he can't be following her. He's probably tracking her by her phone or got a tracking device somewhere on her car."

"I never woulda thought that Camilla would marry a nigga like that," he stated in disbelief.

"That was more so her parents doing but that's a story for another time." Boyce quickly changed the subject. "When you see her, don't mention shit about what I told you. Let her tell you. We haven't told her about you yet even though she did ask about you a couple of times."

"For real?"

"Yeah. I told her that you moved to another state and that you would be down for a visit. I didn't wanna tell her that you were set up and spent six years in jail. I'll leave that up to you."

"Aight. Will she be at the house today?"

"Today is their book club meeting and Camilla always

comes early to help Kia set up. So, if you stick around, you might see her," he grinned.

Turning the music back up, Rafiq nodded his head to YG's "Big Bank' as he thought about everything Boyce told him about Camilla. To say that he was furious about her being married to a sucker ass nigga was an understatement. He always figured that she would be with someone that genuinely cared about her and encouraged her to be the best she could and then some and if they couldn't do that, then they didn't deserve to be with her. Rafiq knew that he couldn't tell Camilla that right away but once he got back in her good graces, he was going to give her the real like he used to do when they were kids.

When they pulled up to the five bedroom, three bathroom house in Marietta, Rafiq nodded his head giving it his stamp of approval.

"I thought we were getting something to eat?" he slid out of the passenger seat.

"We're here," he laughed, "Nakia got everything in there from soul food to seafood in there. We'll hit the mall and the club up later on but right now, it's family time."

"Bet." he smiled, "Aye whose Caddy is this?" He looked inside. "This thang clean."

"Judging by the car seat in the back, it's probably Camilla's," Boyce shrugged.

"She's here? I didn't want her to see me like this, man," Rafiq panicked.

"Nigga calm down. I'm sure she ain't gonna care about that. Now let's get up in here."

Taking a deep breath, he followed his cousin inside the house and the delicious aroma of all sorts of food instantly hit his nose causing his stomach to growl. He admired the fly ass living furniture and the seventy-inch TV that was in the living room as they made their way to the kitchen.

"Aye! Looks who's here?" Boyce moved to the side so Rafiq could be seen.

"Cousin!" Nakia screeched throwing her arms around his neck. "Oh my God! It's so good to have you home!" she kissed his cheek.

"Thanks, Kia." He tightly embraced her. "It's good to be home."

"Bae, who's car is parked in the driveway?"

"That's Camilla's new whip. Her husband got it for her before he went outta town a couple of days ago." She rolled her eyes. "She's putting the kids down for a nap right now."

"That nigga stay buying her something, don't he?" Boyce scoffed.

"Baby, don't get me started." She shook her head.

"Aye. Can I go take a quick shower of something? I need to get this jail stench off me."

"Yeah. Follow me, man."

Rafiq followed Boyce upstairs showing him the guest room with an outfit and a new pair of Timberland boots were waiting for him.

"Did you buy this?" he pointed to the Nike sweat suit and boots on the bed.

"Nakia did." A female voice answered.

The two men turned around, and Rafiq damn near fainted at the sight of the woman before him.

"Camilla?" he looked her up in down in admiration.

"Hey, Rafiq," she smiled, "Long time no see huh?"

"Who you telling?" He gasped.

"Well, are you gonna stand there in a trance or are you gonna give me a hug, big head?"

Without hesitation, Rafiq strolled over to her embracing her tightly. The fragrance she was wearing captivated him causing him to get lost in the moment.

"Cuz, I'ma get you a towel and washcloth." Boyce made his exit leaving them alone.

"It's good to see you again, Rafiq," she softly spoke in his ear.

"Same here." He broke their embrace to look at her. "You've grown into a beautiful woman, Camilla."

"Thank you." She blushed. "And you have grown into a very handsome man. I see you still got that smile that made the girls go crazy when we were kids," Camilla laughed.

He was so wrapped up in her beauty that he didn't hear a word she said.

"Huh? What did you say?"

"Never mind," she chuckled, "I'm gonna let you get washed and dressed. I'll see you downstairs."

"Aight." Rafiq licked his lips.

Watching her walk down the hall, he felt his dick getting hard as he focused on her fat, round ass. Camilla was no longer the petite girl with the bubble butt that he secretly liked. She was a fully-grown, woman and Rafiq was finding it hard to control himself. When Boyce returned with the towel and washcloth, he went into the bathroom, undressed and hopped into the shower. The steamy hot water felt good on his skin as he scrubbed away the stale jail scent that was attached to his body. As thoughts of Camilla ran through his mind, Rafiq's semi-erect dick was rock hard. He thought about all the sexual things he wanted to do to her and found himself beating his meat until he erupted all over the shower wall. That wasn't how he wanted to bust his first nut as a free man, but it was what it was.

Wrapping a towel around his waist, he went into the room and got dressed in the new sweat suit and Timbs that his cousin bought for him. Rafiq grabbed the brush from the dresser and brushed his low-cut fade before putting on the cologne. Examining himself in the mirror, Rafiq smiled at his reflection and mentally prepared himself for the day he had ahead of him but before him and his cousin turned up, Rafiq was going to try to spend as much time with Camilla as possible before they dipped.

## 10

As Camilla sat in her book club meeting, her body was there but her mind was stuck on Rafiq and how sexy he was. His 6'1" frame, athletically built body, light brown eyes and winning smile almost made her forget about her husband as they ate, talked and laughed earlier that day. The four of them reminisced about old times as they stuffed their faces with the delicious food that Nakia prepared for them. Camilla could not stop thinking about how Rafiq teased and tickled her like he used to do when they were kids and even though it was all in fun, she could not help but feel that it might be something more. Learning that Rafiq had spent the last six years of his life in prison upset her because she believed that he was in another state living his life. Although she wanted to know the reason for him being behind bars, she didn't ask. When the men decided to roll out an hour before their book meeting, Camilla became upset because she was not ready for Rafiq to leave but instead of letting her disappointment show, she busied herself with preparing for the meeting.

When the meeting came to an end, the ladies said their good-byes to each other as well as their kids on their way out the door. Closing the door behind them, Camilla and Nakia began cleaning up the minor mess.

"Girl, I can't wait to read the Wife of King Pin." Kia tossed the trash in the bag. "Twyla T and Patrice Balark are some amazing authors. Not to mention J. Dominique and Dani Littlepage. They are my new favorite authors. We can't read no new book until we read everything they wrote."

Camilla continued to clear off the table without saying a word.

"Girl are you listening to me?" she raised her voice a little.

"What?" Camilla snapped out of her thoughts.

"Are you okay, C? You've been out of it all night. You usually have a lot to say during the meeting, but you barely spoke tonight. Wassup?"

"I'm sorry, Kia. My mind has been somewhere else."

"Mmm hmmm," she smirked, "Your mind has been on Rafiq."

"No, it hasn't," Camilla quickly denied.

Nakia burst into a fit of laughter and Camilla joined in.

"You don't know me." she tossed the last of trash in the bag.

"I know you were flirting with that man like you don't have a whole husband." Nakia headed towards the kitchen with Camilla in tow. "If I didn't know any better I would say that someone still has feelings for that man." She glared at her friend.

"Well, I'm glad you do know better because that is not the case and we were not flirting," Camilla pointed out, "We were just playing and having fun. After not seeing each other after all these years, it felt good to see him again," she smiled.

"Yes, it is," Nakia agreed, "My family is finally back together just like mama Jackie wanted it. I still can't believe she's gone."

"I'm so sorry." Camilla rubbed her friends back. "I know that she was special to you. You never did tell me how she passed."

"Someone killed her. Boyce thinks that she was killed because she was trying to get Rafiq out of jail."

"What?" She gasped.

"Mama Jackie believes that Rafiq was set up and was falsely accused of a crime he didn't commit. The lawyers agreed to take his case but before she could tell anyone about it, she was killed. So, Boyce stepped in, worked with the lawyers and when they went through the evidence again, they found that the gun that was used in the murder didn't have Rafiq's fingerprints on it. The people that were involved in this situation confessed to the three murders that were committed, and they've been sentenced to life in prison."

"That's crazy!" Camilla responded in shock, "Who would go through all that trouble to frame Rafiq?"

"I don't know but believe me when I tell you that we're gonna find out," she spoke through gritted teeth. "All mama Jackie wanted to do was get that boy outta jail. Neither of us thought that she would lose her life trying to do so."

"Miss Jackie's death will not be for nothing, Kia. You know I'm always here to help."

"Thanks, C," she smiled. "Instead of you going home, how about you and Kannon spend the night?

"I would love to, but I have to go home and start packing for our trip," she sighed. "Kane told me that when he comes home from his trip, we're finally gonna take our trip to Jamaica."

"The trip that you planned a month and a half ago? The trip that he was too busy to take when you first planned?"

"Mmm hmm." She rolled her eyes. I've never been against him working but these monthly trips are becoming a little too frequent. In the past, he would only be gone for five days at the most but for the past couple of months, he's been gone for two to three weeks at a time. I talk to him every morning and night when he's away, but something seems off, Nakia. Every time he comes home, Kane has gifts for me and Kannon and before he leaves, there are more gifts. I'm glad he eased up and not blowing my phone up or breathing down my neck when I go out now, but after being married to him for nearly five years, I know my husband well enough to know when something isn't right."

"Giirrll, I'm glad you said something about his behavior because I've been dying to say something to you about it," Nakia blurted out.

"Huh? You mean you realized something is off about Kane's behavior too? Why didn't you say anything, Nakia?"

"Because I didn't want to overstep my bounds, Camilla. I haven't seen you in years and the last thing I wanted to do was tell you that you married a control freak that is just like your parents and you needed to take control of your life and push you away. I wanted us to get to know each other again before I started giving you advice."

"You are my best friend and if you see something that I don't, I would like for you to tell me about it, Nakia. You know I've always had a tendency to be naive and a tad bit gullible at times and you always let me know when someone was trying to run game on me because I could never see it for myself," Camilla honestly confessed. "So if I'm missing something, let me know."

"What I'm about to tell you is just my opinion and not facts, but I think your parents persuaded you to marry a man like Kane to keep you sheltered from something. I don't know if it's from the world or whatever secrets they may have but they did it to keep you in the dark about something. Your parents raised you to be an independent woman to be treated with respect and speak up for herself. Not to be controlled by a man and mistreated and for them to tell you to tolerate the bullshit that Kane has put you through over the years is suspect as fuck. Everything your parents have done from the time you were sixteen until now has been for a reason. Now, I'm not telling you to go looking for answers but if you really want them, you're gonna have to do some digging and believe me when I tell you, you may not like what you find," Nakia sincerely spoke.

"You really think my parents might be hiding something?"

"There has to be a reason for them introducing you to Kane when you were seventeen and he was twenty-one. That's statutory rape for real because you weren't eighteen and the fact that they allowed you to date him at that age is suspicious to me and as far as your husband goes, don't be surprised if he's hiding something too. Men give expensive gifts for two reasons. Because it comes from the heart or it's given out of guilt. Which one do you think it is?"

"Well, while we were dating, he used to give me gifts all the time but when we got married, all that shit stopped. Before I bumped into you, he brought me a gift for the first time in years and since then, I've been receiving gifts every month. I thought these gifts were meant to butter me up, but now I'm not so sure," Camilla sighed. "I think I liked shit better when I was oblivious to everything."

"You can only be oblivious for so long, C. It's time for you to wise up." She placed a hand on her shoulder. "But like I said, only go searching for answers if you *really* wanna know the truth."

Taking heed to her best friend's words, Camilla thanked her with a hug before scooping up her purse and Kannon on her way out the door. Nakia walked outside with them to place the trash bags in the can. After strapping her son in his seat, she waited until her bestie was back in the house before backing out of the driveway and headed home. The conversation she had with Nakia was heavily on her mind and even though her friend offered her opinion, Camilla felt like there were some truth to her words. Everything that she said about her parents and Kane made sense to her. Since she was sixteen, her parents, more so her mother told her that everything they did was for her own good which was why they moved to Sandy Springs, ended her friendship with Nakia and pushed her in Kane's direction. At the time, Camilla believed them because her parents never told her anything wrong before but now she felt like everything they did for her was for their benefit and not hers. Camilla wanted to believe that her parents had always been honest with her, but her gut was telling her otherwise. She never questioned them or their methods before and even though she was doubting them, Camilla was afraid to start questioning them now.

Pulling into the driveway of her mansion, she was shocked to see her mother's car parked in her spot. She parked next to her car then unstrapped Kannon from his seat and carried him inside. Before she could unlock the door, it swung open and was greeted by a pissed off Maggie.

"Where the hell have you been child? I've been waiting for you to get home for three hours?"

"Nice to see you to mom," she pushed passed her, "And keep your voice down. My son is sleep." She made her way upstairs to Kannon's room.

"You didn't answer my question, Camilla." Maggie followed behind her.

"If you must know, I was at a book club meeting at Nakia's house," she replied irritably.

"Nakia? Nakia Brown? The little guttersnipe you used to be friends with when you were younger?" She ranted in disbelief.

"My friend is not a guttersnipe, and I need for you to watch what you say about her." She glared at her mom before tucking her son in and leaving the room.

"I will say whatever I want about that raggedy bitch," Maggie spat in disgust.

"Mom, I'm warning you. Don't talk about Nakia like that," she warned as they stood in the hallway.

"What are you doing hanging with her again, Camilla? You don't need someone like her in your life."

"Someone like *her*. What do you mean someone like her?"

"A ghetto hood rat that doesn't have anything going for herself. I bet she still lives in that dirty ass house in Atlanta," Maggie spat.

"Let me tell you something about that ghetto hood rat." Camilla stepped closer to her mother. "That ghetto hood rat is the owner of two successful bakeries, a wife to a loving husband, a mother of two beautiful children, and the best friend a girl like me could have. Unlike the boujie and stuck up bitches you wanted me to hang with, Nakia knew I came from a wealthy family and never asked me for shit. She protected me from people who tried to take advantage of me when we were kids. That ghetto hood rat has a lot more going for herself than I do and she's an example of the woman you raised me to be. So, the next time you fix your lips to say something about Nakia, you better put some respect on her name."

Before Camilla could blink, Maggie slapped her with all her might causing her to grab her face.

"This is exactly why I stopped you from hanging with her. Your outspoken personality and disrespectful attitude you had towards me came from her. She turned you against me back then and I see she's doing the same thing now."

"I like how you blame her for my attitude and feelings towards you, mom. Did you ever stop and think that my relationship with you is tainted because of you? The way that you talk to me and how you want me to be a weak woman by letting my husband control my every move? I feel and treat you the way I do because of you and it makes me wonder why you would want me to tolerate such behavior when you raised me not to."

"Wh--what are you talking about?" Maggie stammered.

"Every time I came to you with a problem, you would just tell me to deal with it. Why is that?"

"Because--I--didn't ---want you to possibly throw away a good thing, Camilla." She dragged. "The issues you were having with Kane weren't serious. It's not like it led to anything physical or degrading."

"But what if it did? Do you know how many women are battered because they tolerated being mistreated, disrespected and abused by their men or husbands just so they could have the finer things in life? Just because Kane hasn't physically or verbally abused me doesn't mean that he won't. I think the only reason you want me to stay with Kane is because he's controlling and manipulative like you are!" She boldly stated.

By the shock expression her mother was wearing on face, Camilla knew that she was taken aback by her words. She had never been that forward with her mother before and she was unsure of how Maggie was going to respond to it. The women glared at each other for a moment until her mother stormed out of the house slamming the door behind her. Not knowing what to think of Maggie's exit, Camilla went back into Kannon's room to get her purse then headed to her bedroom.

Sitting on the edge of the bed, she removed her phone from her purse and when she noticed that Kane did not call her since that morning, Camilla decided to call him, only to get his voicemail. She called him a few more times and got the same result. That was the first time in their relationship that her calls went unanswered from Kane and she didn't know what to make of it. With multiple reasons as to why he didn't answer his phone, Camilla decided to not give it too much thought and try him again in the morning. Placing her phone on the nightstand, she changed into her night shirt and climbed into bed. Instead of thinking about her husband like she usually did, her thoughts drifted to Rafiq as she dozed off to sleep.

## 11
---

As the sun peeked through the blinds, Kane laid in bed with one arm behind his head and the other arm wrapped around Sheena's naked body. Although he had been sleeping with her for the past month, that didn't make the guilt any easier to deal with. Since he agreed to help Sheena more with their daughter, she always found time to FaceTime him, so he could see Kaylynn in the morning before he went to work and at night before he went to sleep. She sent him videos of cute things their daughter did but when she started sending him nude photos of herself, Kane knew that she wanted more than a co-parenting relationship. He had been aware of the signs months ago, but he tried his best to fight the sexual urges that were growing for Sheena but the chemistry was too strong to fight and they ended up in bed together. The more time he spent with Sheena, the more attractive she became to him. Her sex wasn't as good Camilla's but as long as he bust, he didn't give a fuck.

Although Kane enjoyed spending time with Sheena and Kaylynn, he could not stop thinking about Camilla and what she was doing. Since the night he demanded her to come home, she always kept her location off on her phone, so he couldn't track her. Not knowing where Camilla went whenever she left the house drove Kane the fuck crazy, and he couldn't question her about it because she would feel like he was not sticking to his word of not being controlling. However, when he bought her the new silver 2019 Cadillac SUV with a built in navigation system, that put an end to his worrying. Before giving her the car, Kane had a mechanic connect the navigation system in the car to his phone. So, even if Camilla didn't use it, he still knew where she went. He knew what he did was wrong, but he couldn't help himself. Even though he gave his wife his word that he would ease up and agreed for her to live her the way she wanted to, Kane hated that his wife was changing on him, but with the threat of her father looming over him and with the situation he was in with Sheena, Kane's hands were tied.

As he continued to lie in bed, he heard Kaylynn crying down the hall and used that as an opportunity to get out of bed. Grabbing his phone out of his pants pocket, Kane checked his phone on his way down the hall to Kaylynn's room in his boxers and a wife beater. He cussed under his breath when he saw the eight missed calls from his wife. The time that she called him, he was banging Sheena's back out and he couldn't hear his phone ringing over her screaming. As he changed and fed his daughter, Kane thought about the lie he was going to tell Camilla when he called her. After he burped Kaylynn, he carried her down the hall to Sheena's room where he put on a pair of ball shorts then headed downstairs. Placing Kaylynn in her pack n play, he put on Disney Junior and stepped outside on the porch to call Camilla and waited for her to answer.

"Hello, Kane," she answered annoyed.

"Hey, baby," he replied nervously. "Is everything okay?"

"Why didn't you call me last night? I know you saw me calling you?"

"I'm sorry I missed your calls last night, Camilla. I was tired as hell when I got back to my hotel room last night. I was at the building in Philly making sure my team properly set up the software and when I got back to my room, I passed out."

The phone fell silent for a few seconds and Kane's heart began to race.

"Okay, baby," she sighed.

"You don't believe me?"

"I didn't say that. It's just that I'm not used to not hearing from you when you go out of town," Camilla honestly replied.

"I know, baby and believe me when I tell you that it won't happen again, aight?"

"Okay, Kane."

"So, what's on your agenda for the day?"

"I'm going with my friend Nakia to her mentoring program today in College Park. I'm gonna watch how she interacts with young girls and if I like it, I might sign up to be a volunteer myself," she answered cheerfully.

"A mentoring program?" he responded in shock, "Is there anything else you're thinking about doing?"

"I plan on attending college in the fall."

"Say what?"

"You heard right. You know I always wanted to go to school and get my degree. So, I figured now is the time to do so. I already filled out a few applications. I'm just waiting for them to respond."

"Camilla, who put this idea in your head?" Kane couldn't hide his frustration.

"Nobody. I feel like since we're in a better place in our marriage and you've accepted the changes that are being made, why shouldn't I start chasing my dreams and doing the things I've always wanted to do with my life?"

"Look, I dealt with you reuniting with your friend, reading books, joining her book club, you enrolling my son into summer camp and him starting pre-school in September, but this is where I draw the fucking line!" he shouted, "Now you wanna mentor young girls and go to school? This shit is too much, Camilla! With you doing all this shit now, I'll barely have time to see you and my son!"

"Kane, calm down. My classes will be in the morning and I will pick Kannon up from school by 4:30 p.m. You're at work from seven to four and you get home around five. So, we'll still have time to spend together, bae."

"Okay. So, you going to school won't conflict with the time but what about you?"

"What about me?"

"The thought of you going to school and trying to better yourself and shit is bothering me, Camilla," he complained.

"What's wrong with me going to school and trying to better myself, Kane? Don't you want me to do something more with my life than be a boring housewife?"

"No! I want you to be and the stay woman I fucking married! The woman that stayed in the house, didn't ask questions and did what the fuck I told her to do! This is why I was against you going out and hanging with your friend from the beginning. Since you started hanging with that bitch, you started to change and I hate it! I want the old Camilla back! The clueless, naive and sheltered bitch that I married!" Kane shouted.

After ranting out his feelings, he cussed under his breath when Kane realized what he had just said.

"Camilla, baby."

Hearing the phone beep, Kane instantly called Camilla back, but it went straight to voicemail. He called a few more times and got the same result. Tucking his phone in his pocket, he ran his hands over his head as he thought about the mess he made with his wife.

"I see you just keep making shit worse for yourself. Don't you son?" Karl approached the porch with a smile on his face.

"Dad! What the fuck are you doing here?" he stepped off the porch.

"Well, I came out here because one of my old friends, Thomas Walters, invited me to breakfast this morning. I haven't spoken or seen him in months so of course accepted his invitation. Everything was going fine until he showed me a picture of my son, his baby mama and his one-year old daughter." Karl pulled out his phone showing him the picture.

Staring at the picture on his father's phone, Kane swallowed the lump in his throat before responding.

"Dad. I can explain." He held his hands up.

"You can explain? Explain what Kane? How the baby came about? I had that conversation with you when you were twelve!" he spoke through gritted teeth. "Do you know what this could do to you if word got out that you have a child outside of your marriage? Your image and reputation will be ruined!"

"I know that dad. That's why I kept it a secret," Kane confessed, "But I've been taking care of Sheena and Kaylynn the best I could without them knowing the truth about me. She doesn't even know that I'm a successful business man. She just knows that I come from a wealthy family," he shrugged.

"You can't keep hiding them from the world forever Kane and by the conversation you had with your wife, if she hasn't left you already, I'm sure she will once she finds out about this."

"I'm into too deep dad. What the hell am I gonna do?" Kane huffed.

"You told me a couple of months ago to stay out of your personal life. So, that's what I'm gonna do," he smirked. "Enjoy spending time with your... family," Karl turned and walked away.

Kane bit the inside of his cheek as he watched his father get into his car and drive away. He felt some type of way that his father left him hanging in his time of need, but he didn't have anyone to blame but himself. He told his father to stay out his personal life and he was starting to regret telling him that Taking a deep breath, Kane dragged himself back into the house where he saw Kaylynn still in her pack n play and Sheena was in the kitchen preparing breakfast.

"It smells good in here." Kane smiled making his way into the kitchen.

"I figured you must be hungry after the performance you put on last night," Sheena seductively bit her bottom lip.

"Yeah. Last night was amazing." He gripped her hips from behind, kissing her neck.

"Is everything okay? It sounded like you were upset about something when you were outside."

"There is a little trouble back home but nothing that concerns you." Kane took a seat at the table.

The kitchen fell silent for a moment before Sheena spoke again.

"Uh..Kane... I have something to tell you."

"Wassup?"

"My job has asked me to run the Atlanta office for my company but in order for me to work there, I would have to relocate. I already have my mind made up, but I wanted to know how you felt about it." She turned around to face him.

"Running the office for your company in Atlanta sounds like a big deal and you should take it," Kane answered honestly. "Plus, I would be able to see y'all daily instead of monthly."

"I'm glad you feel that way because I was thinking that maybe we could move in with you instead of having the company put me in a house."

"Move in with me? Are you serious?"

"Yes."

"Sheena, I know that things have been going well between

us but I'm not ready to live with you or be in a relationship with you." He stood to his feet.

"What?"

"Don't act like I haven't been telling you this shit all along," he became upset, "Did you think that shit was supposed to change because you're giving me pussy?"

"I thought that we had chemistry, Kane. I thought that we were moving forward and working towards being more than just co-parents," Sheena spoke with disappointment lacing her voice.

"You assumed that shit, Sheena. I never told you that," he sighed. "Look, I can't deny that we have some type of bond, but I can't be with you right now, and us living together is out of the question. I don't mind you relocating to Atlanta for your job, but if you think by you moving closer to me is gonna change my mind, then think again, and just so you won't get any more mixed signals, I'm not spending the night with you anymore whenever I visit you." He stormed out of the kitchen.

"Wait! Where are you going?"

"I got some shit to handle back home."

Stuffing all of his clothes in his suitcase, Kane slid his feet into his Nike slides before snatching up his suitcase and heading down the stairs. He kissed his daughter good-bye then stormed out the door tossing his suitcase in the trunk of his truck.

"Kane, please don't go. I didn't mean to upset you." Sheena ran outside with Kaylynn in her arms.

"I have to go, Sheena, because I did the very thing that I didn't want to do, which was give you false hope and the last thing I wanna do is string you along. I apologize for sending off mixed signals and it won't happen again."

Kane kissed Sheena's forehead and gave his daughter another kiss on her cheek before hopping in his truck, backing out of the driveway and pulling off. As he drove down the expressway, he blew Camilla's phone up hoping that she would answer but his calls kept going straight to voicemail. He didn't doubt for a second that his wife had him on the blocked list but that didn't stop Kane from calling.

When he arrived home, Kane noticed that her car was gone but he was more concerned about her clothes. Parking his car in front of the door, he jumped out, unlocked the front door and rushed upstairs to their bedroom heading straight to the closet. When he saw that most of her clothes were missing, Kane pulled out his phone and began tracking her car. He saw that her car was parked in Marietta and assumed that she was at her friend's house. Kane was ready to drive to where she was and drag her out of there, but he decided to wait and see if Camilla was going to return home on her own and if she didn't, Kane was going to take her by force.

---

## 12

Whe n Camilla showed up at her house a few days prior in tears, Nakia was ready to go to war for her bestie before she even knew what the problem was, but after hearing the hurtful words that her husband had said to her, she was ready to kill Kane. She wanted to make that nigga pay for all the shit that he had put Camilla through over the years but Nakia couldn't react until she gave her the green light. With her friend in need of her support, she was about to skip her mentoring session so she could be by Camilla's side, but she encouraged Nakia to go and when she returned home, the women spent the rest of the evening talking, eating comfort food and binge-watching TV. When they went to bed that night, Nakia thought that her friend was feeling better but when she spent most of her time in her room, she knew that Camilla was really going through it.

Unable to sleep through the night, Nakia laid wide awake in her bed staring at the ceiling. The fact that her bestie was still down in the dumps bothered the hell out of her and she needed to make her feel better. After a couple of hours of thinking and listening to her husband snore, the aroma of bacon invaded her nose. Tossing the blanket off of her, Nakia stuffed her feet in her slipper and headed to the kitchen where she saw Camilla cooking breakfast.

"Aye, C."

"Hey, Kia," she solemnly replied "Have a seat. I made breakfast for everybody."

"Camilla, it's 6:05 in the morning. Ain't it a lil early for breakfast?"

"I know but I haven't eaten anything in the past couple of days. So I decided to cook for everyone." She prepared their plates.

Placing a plate in front of her, Nakia thanked her before silently blessing her food and digging in. When she noticed that Camilla wasn't eating, she put her fork down.

"What's on your mind, C?"

"Do you know I have nothing to my name, Kia? Everything that I own was provided by Kane. The car, my clothes, my phone, the house and the money he gives me is all him. I was thinking about what I would do or where I would go if I left him and the only place I could go is my parents' house and I'll be damned if I go there because I can't stand my mom," she huffed, "I really fucked my life up, Nakia."

"You know that you and Kannon can stay with us as long as y'all need to."

"I appreciate that Nakia, but we can't stay here. We've only been here for a few days and I already feel like a freeloader," she sighed, "I was trying to figure out how I could survive on my own and the option I have is to move back home, save the money that Kane gives me and when I get enough, I can leave his ass for good."

"Or you can apply to colleges like you planned, get a job and start making your own money or both," Nakia boldly stated, "You don't need that nigga to take care of you Camilla.

You can take care of yourself and your son on your own and you already know I'm here for you."

"That sounds good and everything, but you know I don't have any skills. I never worked a day in my life."

"How about you work at the bakery with me?"

"What?"

"Yeah. I'm hiring employees for my newest bakery in Mableton, and since I'm running that store by myself for right now, I can train you on everything you need to know, and of course I'll pay you," she explained. "So, what do you say?"

"I guess I can give it a try." She smirked.

"Great! Now, when you start applying for schools, you can use my address. So that husband of yours won't know what you're up to and since you won't stay here, I think you should talk to your dad and see if he can help you get a new car and a place to stay."

"I think you're right, Kia." She nodded. I haven't talked to my dad in a while and I'm pretty sure he doesn't know what's going on with me and Kane. I just hope he doesn't try to persuade me to stay with his like my mom does."

"Ya mama is a piece of work child."

"Tell me about it. When I went home on Wednesday, she was at my house waiting for me and when I told her that I was hanging out with you, she lost it." Camilla shook her head.

"I'm sure she was talking mad shit about me."

"Yeah. She was but I checked her ass for talking you about like that and she ended up slapping me."

"Damn. She slapped you for defending me?" Nakia gasped.

"That and the way I was talking to her. She blames you for my attitude towards her and my outspoken demeanor, but I told her that you have nothing to do with my feelings towards her. My mother has a problem with taking responsibility for her own shit and she blames everyone else for their problems with her." Camilla shook her head.

"I appreciate you sticking up for me C, but I don't want you beefing with your mom because of me."

"It's cool. We haven't been close for years now. I don't know what changed in my mother, but I need to figure out why she is the way she is. I don't see how my dad puts up with her." She shook her head again.

"Neither do I," she agreed. "We should start getting ready for work. The bakery opens at nine."

"I'm starting today?"

"Unless you got something else to do."

"Well, let me start getting ready."

Laughing at her friend, Nakia finished her food before washing her plate and headed to her bedroom to get ready for her day. Once she was washed and dressed, she got her kids ready for camp and Camilla did the same with Kannon. After the kids were fed, the ladies headed out the house and Boyce watched them as they placed the kids in the back of Nakia's white 2019 Lexus SUV. As the women were about to get into the car, A black truck pulled up and blocked the driveway. When Nakia noticed the terrified look on Camilla's face, she knew that had to be the infamous Kane Jacobs.

"Camilla, I didn't come here to cause a scene." He hopped out the truck leaving the door open. "Just get your shit, put my son in the car and lets go," Kane spoke sternly.

"How did you know I was here, Kane?"

"Don't worry about that. Now do what I told you to do so we can go."

"Me and my son ain't going nowhere with you, "she spat, "Now that I know how you really feel about me and what type of wife you want me to be, I'm never coming back home."

"Where the fuck are you gonna go huh? What the fuck are you gonna do Camilla? You won't survive without me and you know it! Without me, you won't be shit but an average bitch and live an average life like these average ass motherfuckers you're hanging with," he smirked, "Now get the fuck in the car and stop playing with me!"

"Oh hell naw! Who the fuck you calling average you weak ass motherfucker?" Nakia walked towards him but Boyce pulled her back.

"My man, Camilla said she ain't going with you. So, you need to roll before shit gets ugly out here," Boyce stepped in front of Nakia.

"Nigga this shit is between me and my wife. So, mind your fucking business." Kane looked him up and down.

"Get the fuck outta her Kane. I said I ain't going with you. Now leave me the fuck alone!"

Without hesitation, Kane charged towards Camilla, but Boyce stopped him in his tracks with a three-piece combo that sent him flying to the ground. Nakia and Camilla watched as Boyce climbed on top of Kane and delivered blow after blow to his face. Realizing that her husband wasn't going to let up, Nakia ran over pulling him off of Kane.

"Now get the fuck off our property bitch ass nigga." She spoke through gritted teeth as she held Boyce back.

They watched as a bloody Kane slowly rose to his feet climbing inside his truck.

"This shit ain't over, Camilla," he warned before he pulled off.

As he peeled off down the block, Nakia saw that Camilla was trembling with fear. Walking over to her, she hugged her friend to calm her down.

"Calm down, Camilla. Everything is gonna be aight."

"I.. I can't believe he was really gonna put his hands on me," she stated in shock. "He was gonna put his hands on me in front of our son. I can't believe this." She began to cry. "I didn't mean to bring this drama to y'all doorstep. I'm so sorry y'all. Camilla sniffled. "I don't know how he found me."

"It was probably the car, Camilla. It might have some type of tracking device on it," Boyce answered.

"Oh my God," she gasped, "He promised me that he'd changed, and he hasn't changed a bit. That was the reason he gave me the car in the first place. So, he could keep tabs on me, I can't believe his lying ass," she choked out."

"Camilla, you've been through a lot this morning. How about you start your training some other time?"

"No. I still wanna start today. If I'm gonna change my life, I need to start as soon as possible. I'll be aight. Let's go." She wiped her tears away.

"Look, y'all take my truck and I'll drop the kids off in the SUV. Just in case this nigga tries to pull up and do some goofy shit." Boyce handed Nakia his car keys and Nakia did the same.

"Thank you for sticking up for me Boyce."

"No need to thank me. Your family and family protect each other."

After Camilla gave Boyce a quick hug, the ladies kissed their kids good-bye and hopped inside the navy blue 2019 Hummer truck. As Nakia headed to the bakery, she kept glancing at her bestie to make sure she was cool, and Camilla seemed to be okay. She was doing something on her phone and she hoped that she was texting her father. Nakia was surprised that she still wanted to go to work with her but that showed her just how determined Camilla was to start her new life and as her friend, Nakia was going to do everything possible to help her friend be successful. She just hoped that Camilla could handle being a working woman and not return to the easy but miserable life she once had.

## 13

A few days had passed since the incident that happened at Nakia's house and Camilla was still shaking with fear. Every time she closed her eyes, she thought about the demonic look that was displayed on Kane's face when he tried to attack her, and she could not get that image out of her head. The nightmares she had about him attacking her kept her from sleeping but that didn't stop her from going to work with Nakia and monitoring her at her mentoring program that day. A few of the girls noticed Camilla from a photo in a business magazine that was taken of her and her family at the businessman of the year award ceremony. The girls asked for her autograph and a bunch of questions about life. Like what's it like being married to a Boss and what do they have to do to catch a man like Kane. Camilla was taken aback by the questions the young girls were asking her because Nakia was teaching them how to be independent women and all they wanted to do is land a great catch and have the easy life. Instead of answering their questions, she ran out of the building in tears.

Even though Camilla was taking the steps to create a life of her own, she felt like everything she was doing was for nothing. The college applications she filled out along with the effort she showed getting out of bed every day felt like it was a waste of time. The life that she wanted to create for herself was the life that she had with Kane, and her trying to reach the status he was at was damn near impossible for her to do on her own. With his words echoing in her head that she wouldn't be shit without him, it was slowly destroying all of the confidence that Nakia had given her to move on and start living her life the way she wanted to. After learning that her husband viewed her as naive, sheltered and clueless, Camilla knew that it would be weak of her to go back to him and even though he tried to attack her, she still had love for the man that thought so little of her.

After an hour of sitting in her car, Nakia jumped behind the wheel slamming the door closed.

"Aye, Camilla, are you aight? I didn't know that the girl knew who you were," she spoke sincerely.

"I don't mind that they noticed me. I didn't even know that my pictures were in the magazine. I mean, I know that Kane is wealthy and everything, but I never viewed him as a boss," she wiped her tears."

"That's because you were with him before he became who he was, C I didn't know who he was until I looked his ass up the other day and I hate to say this, but your husband is a big deal in the city of Atlanta, just like his pop and Mr. Richard are. Most would say that you would be a fool to walk away from a nigga like that and I'm hoping that you're willing to be a fool, Camilla."

"To be honest Kia, I don't know if I'm willing to take that chance."

"Say what?"

"Kane is all that know, and I know that he's controlling and has some issues, but he is still my husband and the father of my son. I know it may sound crazy, but I love him, and I don't know if I'm ready to give him or this life up just yet." She looked at her friend.

"Camilla, are you serious right now? That nigga woulda beat ya ass if Boyce wouldn't have stepped in. That nigga put a tracking device on ya car, so he can tabs on you. That nigga don't love you. He loves what you look like and the fact that you're young, naive, clueless and sheltered, that just makes it easy for him to control you. I know that Kane has provided you with a glamorous life Camilla, but is it worth losing yourself for it?"

Camilla took a minute to think about an answer.

"It shouldn't be but I gotta be realistic Kia. I'm never gonna be able to maintain this lifestyle on my own. He was right when he said that I won't survive without him."

"Yes you will and you can but if you don't believe in yourself, you will constantly be paralyzed by fear. I understand you want to make your marriage work but don't go back to that nigga until he makes an effort to change his ways because if you go back to him now, he's gonna keep you away from all the positive things in your life. You done filled out college apps, you're doing well at the bakery, your son is livelier and more active, you're not as closed off as you once were. You've come a long way in a short period of time, C. Please don't go back to the woman you used to be," Nakia pleaded.

"I won't, Nakia," she smiled. "I know I how negative thoughts about myself, but I don't wanna go back to being a boring ass housewife. I just don't have the ability to hustle like you do. I need things to happen overnight."

"There are no elevators to success, sis. You gotta take the stairs."

Camilla nodded her head in understanding as Nakia crunked up the car and headed to her house to pick up Kannon then she dropped him off at her parents' house in Sandy Springs.

"Daaammmnn! Ya folks done upgraded to a mansion? This is the crib y'all moved to when you were sixteen?" she asked with wide eyes.

"Yeah," Camilla chuckled, "If you think this is nice, you should see the mansion I shared with Kane."

"Damn! You lived in a mansion too?"

"Mmm hmm."

"Shit! Now I see why you're willing to deal with that man and his bullshit," Nakia joked.

"Shut up Kia," she laughed, "Thanks for dropping us off. Depending on how this conversation goes, I might be catching an uber back to you crib."

"I don't mind picking y'all up. Just hit my line when you're ready."

"Okay. Thanks Kia." she hugged her friend.

Hopping out of the car, Camilla unstrapped Kannon from his seat then headed inside the mansion.

"Daddy?" she called out.

"I'm in my office, baby girl," Richard replied.

Kannon took off down the hall as she followed behind her son.

"There's my favorite grandson," he smiled as Kannon jumped in his lap.

"I'm your only grandson, grandpa." He giggled.

"Hey, dad." Camilla walked around the desk to hug him.

"Hey, baby girl." He kissed her cheek. "You know I was kind of surprised when you said you wanted to talk to me. You usually talk to your mom whenever you have problems."

"Kannon baby. Go sit over there on the couch and play with your iPad." Camilla removed the device from her purse and handed it to him.

"Okay mommy."

"I know I usually talk to mom," she sat down in one of the office chairs, "But after she slapped me a few nights ago during an argument we were having, I don't have no words for her."

"Maggie slapped you? What was the argument about?"

"I'll get into that later but I'm here to talk to you about Kane."

"What about him?" Richard's jaws got tight.

Camilla started from the beginning with the issues that she was having with Kane and the life he had her living. She informed him about all the times he shut down her ideas of wanting to do things and his controlling way. Camilla told him how Kane reacted when she told him about Nakia and the book club to the most recent events of him trying to attack her. She explained to her father the feelings she has for her husband and how she wanted their marriage to work. By the time Camilla finished giving Richard the rundown, he had his stainless steel Chinese massage balls in his hand. The only time her father used those was when he was extremely pissed and needed to calm down. The office was silent for a moment before Richard spoke.

"Your mother knew he was treating you like this and just told you deal with it?"

"Yes, sir, and that's why I came to you."

"And what was the argument about that y'all had the other day?"

"She was waiting for me at my house when I came home from my book club meeting. I told her I was with Nakia, and she instantly bashed her. I told her not to talk about her in that manner and when I told her that Nakia is an example of the woman she wanted me to be, mom slapped me. She blamed Nakia for my ill feelings towards her, and once I explained that Nakia had nothing to do with the way I feel about her and told her that Kane is controlling like she is, mom stormed out of the house."

"Hmm. Your mom always had a thing against that girl. She convinced me that Nakia was a bad influence on you but I never felt like she was. Yeah, she was a little ghetto and rough around the edges, but that girl had your best interests at heart. Every time you tried to give her money or give her something of yours, Nakia always turned you down and I admire that about her. Your mom said that she had you hanging with the wrong crowd but instead of me investigating things for myself, I took her word for it and moved you away from her," Richard confessed, "I'm glad that she's back in your life. You need positive people around you that gonna protect you and have your back."

Camilla was shocked by her fathers' words. Unable to speak, she remained silent and let him finish talking.

"I told that husband of yours that if he didn't start doing right by you, I was gonna make sure you divorced his ass and take him for everything he had. Your mother tried to convince me to agree that you needed to deal with his shenanigans, but I refused. I knew that nigga wasn't ready to marry you but since Karl gave me his word that Kane was gonna do right by you, I trusted him with my most prized possession only for the lil nigga to mistreat you."

"Oh Daddy." her eyes filled with tears.

"I didn't stand up for you when I was supposed to Camilla and I apologize for that but now, I'm gonna be the father I shoulda been seven years ago. I know you still love Kane and I understand that you wanna work on your marriage, but you shouldn't make the first move. He fucked up. Therefore, he should be coming up with a solution to get y'all back on track. If he really wants to be with you, he'll do whatever is needed to get you back," Richard sternly stated, "Don't keep Kane away from his son. If he wants to spend time with Kannon, he can pick him up from here. The only time y'all should communicate is if it concerns y'all son or something pertaining to marriage counseling, if Kane suggest that. As far as the car he gave you, have it towed back to the mansion. You can have one of my cars. We'll get the title, and everything switched tomorrow and you can stay at one of the properties I have in a cul-de-sac not too far from here."

With tears rolling down her cheeks, Camilla was overwhelmed by the things that her father said to her. For the longest time, Richard followed her mother's lead and didn't protest but to hear him say that he was going to be the father he should've always been and the way he was helping her out, was more than Camilla expected from her father.

"Thanks, dad." She sniffled. "You don't know how much this means to me."

"You're my only daughter, Camilla, and I'm gonna show you what a man is supposed to be and how he's supposed to treat a woman." He smiled at her. "And I have to say that I'm proud of you."

"For what?" She dried her eyes.

"Because you started living your life. I'm happy that you applied for school, you're learning skills and interacting with people. There is so much more to life than being a housewife and I'm glad that you decided to break free from Kane and not listen to your mother." He rose to his feet and walked around the desk.

Standing to her feet, Camilla tightly embraced her father as more tears fell from her eyes. Breaking their embrace, her father guided her and Kannon outside to his garage where he let Camilla choose from the five cars he had stored there. When Kannon admired the 2019 pearl blue Mercedes Benz, she fell in love with it. Richard quickly dashed inside and returned with the car key, the keys to her new house, and a few credit cards that had her name on them. The confused expression on her face made him chuckle, so he explained.

"When I thought you were going off to college, I ordered

these for you but when you changed your mind, I just held them for you. You have a good credit score, so you can get whatever you want, but until you fully get on your feet, you can use these until you feel as though you don't need them anymore. Until then, I got you."

"Oh, dad. This is too much."

"This is me making up for lost time," he sighed. "I haven't spoiled you in a long time. So, let me start doing it again." Richard gave a small smile. "Now I texted you the address to the house. Let me know when you get there."

"Okay, dad."

Grabbing the spare car seat, Camilla jumped behind the wheel of her new whip and started the engine while Richard strapped his grandson in. She hugged and kissed father goodbye before pulling out of the driveway and heading to her new house that was thirty minutes away from her parents' home. Parking in the driveway, Camilla did a quick scan of her surroundings as she helped her son out of the car. Unlocking the front door to her new home, her mouth hit the floor at the sight of the beautifully decorated and spacious home. The seventy-five-inch smart tv was mounted to the wall and the chocolate-colored sofa and recliner matched the brown carpet that covered the living room floor. As Kannon ran upstairs, Camilla examined the kitchen with the updated stainless-steel appliances. Going into the basement, she loved that it was finished and thought about turning it into a play area for Kannon or use it to host the book club meetings. She headed upstairs and past three bedrooms and a bathroom before she reached the master bedroom where she found Kannon jumping on the bed.

"I like our new house Mommy." He flopped down on the bed.

"I'm glad you like it son." She sat down next to him.

"Is daddy gonna live here with us?"

"No. Daddy is gonna stay at the mansion."

"Good." He nodded.

"Why you say that, Kannon?"

"Because daddy was mean to you the other day and when we were at the old house, you weren't very happy and I want you to be happy, mommy."

"And we will be, baby."

Scooping her son up in her arms, Camilla kissed his forehead and hugged him tightly. She didn't think that he was paying attention to Kane's fuckery or the fact that she was unhappy at the mansion, but she was very wrong. Now that she was aware that her son was paying more attention to her than she thought, Camilla had to be careful of the things her son saw and heard from that point on.

After spending the last few days unsure of what she wanted to do with her life, Nakia's pep talk along with her father's help restored her confidence in herself. Although she was still in the process of finding herself, Camilla decided to use her status as the wife of a boss to her advantage like the rest of the women did. Determined to make up for the miserable years being married to Kane Jacobs, she was going to make the rest of her time married to him worth something, even if they didn't stay married.

## 14

Nearly three weeks had passed since Kane pulled up on Camilla and to say that he was going crazy would be an understatement. After Nakia's husband whooped his ass he spent the rest of the day in the house cleaning up his bruises. He blew his wife's phone up hoping that she removed him from the block list, but he still got the voicemail every time he called her. Kane checked the navigation system on the car he got for her and when the car had not moved from Nakia's house in days, he realized that she was no longer driving the car. When he was on his way home from work one day, Kane checked the navigation system and saw that the car was parked at their house. He was so excited that Camilla came to her senses and returned home but when he reached the house and saw that she wasn't there, he had a fucking tantrum. He searched the car and found the clothes she packed along with her phone which were all the things he brought inside of it. Her house and car keys were inside as well. By Camilla returning everything that he had bought her, and the keys, Kane took that as her way of telling him fuck you. Kane was not happy about that shit at all.

As he waited for his bruises to heal, Kane remained in the house where he worked from home during the day and drowned his sorrows with Henny during the night. All he did was think about Camilla and his son. Kane tried to convince himself that he didn't miss or need his wife, but he was just lying to himself. Although he provided her with a glamorous yet sheltered life, he knew that Camilla was capable of being successful at anything she chose to do with her life. Even when she was seventeen, she knew how to talk to people, and both men and women gravitated towards her. Kane noticed that she was a strong woman and that intimidated the hell out of him because he didn't know how to handle a woman who didn't need him for anything but instead of leaving her alone to live her life and follow her dreams, Kane couldn't stand the thought of seeing her with anyone else. So, he married her, killed her confidence, stopped her from being opinionated and kept her from the outside world. Kane knew he was an ain't shit nigga from the beginning, but his pride wouldn't allow him to admit it. Knowing that he was better off letting her go, Kane wasn't ready to get divorced from his wife. He badly wanted her back, but he wasn't sure if he was going to do right by her if he ever got the chance.

As he sat at the kitchen counter eating Kannon's Reese Puffs, his ringing phone interrupted the game he was playing. Seeing his dad's name on his screen made his mood even worse. He didn't want to answer the call, but he thought that it was business-related.

"Yo, dad."

"Damn. You sound like you're going through it over there. You aight?"

"No, but I'll manage. Wassup."

"Business, son. I need you here asap."

"I'll be there."

Ending the call, Kane dragged his ass upstairs and got in

the shower. That was his first time washing his ass in a couple of days, so he stayed in the shower a little longer than usual. After he finished washing, he threw on one his tailored made suits, a pair of Christian Louboutin dress shoes and his presidential Rolex. Snatching up his keys, wallet and phone, Kane left the house and hopped in his truck. Pulling out of the driveway, he maneuvered through the streets of Atlanta mentally preparing himself for the business meeting. When he arrived at his father's house minutes later, he saw Richard's car and another he didn't recognize. Parking in his usual spot, Kane took a deep breath before entering the house. He made his way down the hall to his father's office and saw Richard, Maggie, Thomas and his dad with serious expressions on their faces. He locked eyes with Thomas who was glaring at him like he wanted to kill him. His father signaled him to stand beside him and Kane hesitated a little before taking his place next to his dad.

"Kane, I know you I told you that this was a business meeting but this ain't our usual one." Karl stood to his feet. "When Thomas called me with a proposition, I told him that he needed to come meet me so we could discuss some things in person and when Richard and Maggie showed up with some concerns about you, I told them to come over as well. Now that we're all here, whoever wants to start the meeting my take the floor."

"I'll start." Thomas rose to his feet. "I called Karl so we could discuss the possibility of you and Sheena being together and what I had to do to make that happen but when she called me in tears telling me that you have a wife that she knew nothing about, I damn near crashed my car!" Thomas roared.

"Excuse me." Maggie raised her hand. "Who is Sheena?" She looked from Thomas to Karl then to Kane.

"Go head and answer her, Kane?" Thomas glared at him.

"Sheena...is my...daughter's mother." He answered shamefully.

"What!" Maggie jumped to her feet.

"You mean to tell me that you cheated on my daughter and had a baby on her?" Richard spoke through gritted teeth. "Nigga, I oughta whoop ya ass!" He tried to charge towards him but Maggie and Karl held him back.

"How could you do this, Kane?" Maggie shook her head in disgust.

"Now I understand why you could never be with my daughter and grandchild." Thomas scoffed, "And I thought you were an upstanding young man but you're just like the rest of these ain't shit niggas."

"Now that we have everything out in the open, let's discuss a solution to this problem." Karl stayed by Richard's side.

"I want Kane to stop keeping my daughter and grandchild a secret." Thomas spoke up. "My daughter was deceived by this man, and if he doesn't come out publicly with this, we'll take his ass to court for child support."

"Mr. Walters, I understand that you're upset finding out the truth about me this way, but I can't go public with this shit. It will destroy me and my marriage." Kane panicked. "Can't we come to some type of agreement privately?"

"I gotta see what my daughter wants to do but when my daughter moves here next week, you better spend as much time as you can with my granddaughter, and if Sheena tells me that you haven't been helping her take care of that child, I'll go public with this shit myself."

The men stared each other down until Thomas walked out of the office. Putting his focus on Maggie and Richard, his heart was damn near pounding out of his chest.

"I came here to tell you the conditions Camilla had in order for you to see Kannon and to let you know that she wants y'all marriage to work, but you had to make the first move but after hearing this, I'm not sure I want you anywhere near my daughter." Richard sternly stated.

"Mr. Richard, I don't mean no disrespect, but this is me and Camilla's marriage, and y'all really have nothing to do this."

"That's where you're wrong Kane." He stepped closer to him. "When my daughter came to me and told me the things you did to her, it became *my* business. I trusted you with my daughter and you mistreated, controlled and cheated on her. Now I know my daughter has the final say at the end of the day but I just want you to know that no matter what you do, I will never forgive you for this shit. Business is always business but outside of that, I don't want anything to do with you. Karl, call me later so we can discuss the next moves for Maryland and New York."

Richard left the office with Maggie on his heels. Hearing the front door close, Kane took a seat burying his face in his hands.

"Looks like you created quite a mess, son." Karl sat back behind his desk.

"I didn't want them to find out this way," he sighed. "And how the hell did Sheena even find out about Camilla?"

"Camilla has a commercial out for a bakery she works at and in the commercial, she says that she is your wife," he chuckled. "I gotta hand it to her. That girl knows how to advertise. Since this commercial came out, that bakery has been the talk of the town."

"She's working at a bakery? Where the hell did she get the money for the commercial? Camilla doesn't have shit!"

"She has parents, Kane, and a father that is determined to see her succeed. Now that she's on her own, she is doing better than she ever could. You were holding her back Kane. So, my suggestion, even though I know you don't want it, is to leave her be. Y'all can still be married but be apart. Maybe that will allow you to get ya shit together and when you feel as though you're ready to have her back, suggest counseling and see where it goes from there." Karl calmly replied.

"But the more time I spend away from her, Camilla might not want me anymore. She's only been away from me for a month and she's already doing commercials for a bakery she's working at," Kane stated in disbelief. "I told that girl that she wouldn't be able to survive without me but she's proving me wrong."

"I guess she's surrounding herself with positive people who bring out the best in her and not dim her light like you did." Karl smirked.

"So, what do I do about Sheena?"

"If you don't want her to spill the beans about your affair, you can either deal with her terms, go public or tell Camilla yourself."

"I guess I have some things to think about." Kane stood to his feet. "Thanks for the advice, dad."

"No problem, son. I'll talk to you later."

Kane left out of the house, hopped in his truck and pulled off. As he headed home, a call came through on his phone and when he saw that it was Sheena, he reluctantly answered.

"Hello, Sheena," he tried to hide his irritation.

"Kane," replied angrily, "You know you coulda told me from the jump that you were a married man. I woulda left ya ass alone."

"What the fuck do you want me to do, Sheena? Apologize? That shit ain't gonna fix what happened between us. I know I shoulda kept it real with you from the jump, but I didn't expect the condom to break or for you to get pregnant. So, tell me what the fuck you want."

"I want the life your wife has."

"What?"

"You heard me. I want the nice ass crib, the fly ass whip,

designer clothes, all that shit," she demanded. "If you want me to keep my mouth shut, these are my terms."

"So, I guess you're gonna quit ya job and live off me?"

"You damn right! Now that I know you're one of the bosses of Atlanta, I'm gonna take advantage of the shit. This upcoming week is my last week of work, and I'll be in Atlanta on Monday by noon. That's more than enough time to have my house ready, and I'll pick out my car when I get there."

When the call ended, Kane tossed his phone in the passenger seat and drove like a mad man the rest of the way home. Sheena's plans to quit her job and live off of him had him livid. He always thought of her as a hardworking, independent woman and was comfortable with earning her own money, but learning the truth about her in the matter of seconds frustrated him. He didn't want to take care of that bitch. The only person Kane was comfortable taking care of was his wife and no one else. Arriving home a few seconds later, he went straight to the kitchen, cracked open a bottle of whiskey and took a huge gulp from the bottle. With Camilla doing well on her own and Sheena extorting him for money, Kane didn't know how he was going to manage, but until he figured shit, alcohol would be his best friend.

## 15

"That's so fucked up Rafiq," the blond hair bitch whined, "How are you just gonna leave me her with no way to get home?"

"Bitch you a stripper and with all the money you made tonight, you got a fucking way to get home," he tossed over his shoulder getting in his truck, "Oh and you need to tighten up ya pussy. That shit a lil loose ma."

"Fuck you, you lame ass nigga!" she yelled as he pulled out of the hotel parking lot

Rafiq laughed to himself as he turned his music up and headed towards the expressway to his apartment in Austell. He was amused at how bitches threw the pussy at him and expected him to pay for the shit. They had him all the way fucked up. Although he knew the rules of the game, Rafiq didn't play by the rules. He had been fucking and ducking bitches since he came home from prison and all the bitches he fucked were just substitutes for the one he really wanted. Camilla. Since he saw her at his cousin's house the day he was released, he could not get her off his mind. Rafiq wanted to spend more time with her when she was staying at Boyce's crib but he was busy helping his cousin get his business up and running. When his cousin told him about the incident with Camilla and her husband, he was ready to go to war for shawty. He couldn't understand for the life of him why she was still with that nigga and that was a question he was going to be sure to ask her.

When he arrived at his apartment complex, Rafiq punched in the code to unlock the gate and he drove through. Making a few twists and turns, he pulled in the nearest spot, killed the engine then jumped out of his truck. Jogging up the stairs to his apartment, he unlocked the door walking inside and flopping down on the couch. Between working with Boyce in the day time and hoeing at night, Rafiq was beyond tired and within seconds he was passed out. It only seemed like he was sleep for only a few minutes before his phone began to ring waking him up out of sleep. Removing his phone from his pocket, he answered it with his eyes still closed.

"Who this?" he grumbled.

"You sound ugly as fuck in the morning," the female giggled on the other end.

"Camilla?" His eyes popped opened.

"Yeah boy."

"Oh shit. I wasn't expecting to hear from you." Rafiq sat up on the couch. "Boyce must've given you my number."

"Nah. I'm calling you from his phone. Listen, we're about to spend the day turning up like we used to. My son is with my folks and their kids are spending the day with one of the ladies from our book club. So, it'll just be the four of us like old times. So, get the funk off your breath, get fresh and get your ass over here."

"Say no more," he chuckled. "I'll be there within the hour."

Ending the call with a grin on his face, Rafiq jumped up from the couch and headed to his master bathroom where he got into the shower. As he washed up, he reminisced about all of the things they used to do whenever they linked up. They used to travel everywhere on the Marta bus and even though they got lost most of the time, they always found their way back home. Whenever they would hit up the mall or went out to eat the one thing Rafiq wanted to do was spend money on Camilla. He knew it wouldn't matter much to her because she came from money but all he wanted to do was spoil her and show her a good time. He wasn't sure if he was going to get a chance to do that, but he was hoping that she would let him.

Once he was finished in the bathroom, he threw on fresh pair of Polo boxers and wife beater along with a pair of light denim Balmain shorts, red Versace shirt and his custom made white low top Air Force Ones with the Versace pattern on the swoosh. Putting on his gold chain and big face Rolex, Rafiq stood in the mirror brushing his hair. The cocky smile he gave himself as he put on his smell goods confirmed what he already knew. That he was a sexy motherfucker. Removing a few stacks from his safe in the closet, Rafiq carefully tucked them in his pocket before snatching up his keys and phone from the couch on his way out the door. He popped the locks to the money green Lincoln Navigator his cousin gave him, jumped behind the wheel, revved the engine, then drove off. Arriving at his cousin's house minutes later, he couldn't stop the smile that spread across his face. Not only was Boyce's outfit similar to his but Camilla and Nakia were dressed exactly the same like they used to do when they were kids. From their high ponytails down to their all white shell toe Adidas. The only difference was that they were grown now and not the overdeveloped teens they used to know.

"I see we were all thinking alike huh?" Rafiq hopped out of his car with the engine running.

"Yeah. I guess so," Boyce chuckled while giving him a hand-shake, "But don't this shit right here bring back memories though?" He pointed to the girls.

"Damn sure does." he seductively eyed Camilla making her blush.

"C almost fucked up our outfits," Nakia scoffed, "Talking about the shorts are too short,"

"I'm not used to wearing shit like this. My husband always bought my clothes and he always had me covered up," she tugged at her thigh lengths shorts. "I feel naked."

Rafiq's face twisted up into a frown after hearing Camilla's words.

"Take it from me sis, if there was a problem with y'all outfits, I woulda pulled Kia to the side and put a bug in her ear because all that having ya ass hanging out the bottom of your shorts and titties on displayed is a no go," Boyce stated, "So from a married man's point of view, you're good sis."

"Thanks B." She smiled.

"Aight. So where are we going first? Nakia rubbed her hands together.

"How about we start the day off at Six Flags?" Boyce suggested.

"Sounds good to me," the ladies responded in unison.

"Rafiq, you good?" Boyce asked causing all eyes to be on him.

"Yeah. I'm good. I'm down with Six Flags."

"Cool. C how about you ride Rafiq so you won't have to drive?" Nakia suggested.

"Okay." She hesitantly replied.

Boyce helped Nakia inside of his truck while Rafiq helped Camilla inside of his. Closing the for her, he jumped behind the wheel and pulled off. Although he did his best to hide his mood from Camilla, it was becoming damn near impossible for him to do. He had so many questions running through his head and so many things he wanted to say to her, but he didn't want his words to come out wrong. Tired of the awkward silence between them, Rafiq spoke his mind.

"Can I ask you something?"

"Go head?"

"Why did you marry that nigga Kane?"

"What?"

"Why did you marry him? Because if he's as controlling as you say he is, why would you marry a nigga like that, let alone stay with him?"

"Kane wasn't always like that. When we first started dating, he catered to my needs, listened to my opinions and showered me with gifts and I ended up falling in love with him. Plus, my parents approved of him but as soon as our honeymoon was over, Kane instantly changed. At first I thought it was cute how he bought my clothes and checked on me while I was out and suggested that I work out and watched what I ate but when he started talking to me crazy, telling me shit like speak when spoken to and shutting me down every time I voiced my opinion. I knew I had to leave but my mom convinced me that things would get better but better never came. I thought he was getting better because he was doing the things that he used to do in the beginning but everything he got me was out of guilt," she paused, "I don't think that nigga ever really loved me. I just think he wanted me because he didn't want no else to have me and did whatever was needed to get me. I was young, stupid and naive and I've been like that for most of my life, but I refuse to stay that way."

Rafiq glanced over at her and saw Camilla wiping her eyes. Learning the reason for her decision to marry that asshole made him feel like shit for thinking that she willingly married that nigga on her own but the reality of it was that she was manipulated into doing so by the people she trusted the most. He hated that her parents and Kane took advantage of her and he was going to make sure that no one did that shit again.

"When was the last time you seen ole boy?"

"The day Boyce whooped his ass for lunging towards me," she laughed.

"Yeah. He told me about that. Said that boy shit was leaking something oorious "

"Like a damn faucet was running."

They erupted in laughter.

"Damn. So, it's been like a month now."

"Yup."

"Are you gonna go back to him?" He glanced at her.

Camilla locked eyes with him for a few seconds before shifting her eyes to the floor.

"To be honest Rafiq, I don't know. When I left him, I thought about going back to him because I didn't think I could make it without him and I still had love for him but now that I realized he probably never loved me from the beginning and I'm doing fine without him, I strongly believe that our marriage is over."

"For real?"

"Yeah. I mean I'm still finding my way but now that I have my friends and my dad in my corner, I can do no wrong. I deserve to be treated like a queen and not a prisoner. I can do anything I put my mind to and I will not let anyone hold me back any longer."

"That's the Camilla I know and love," he smiled."

By the shocked expression on her face, Rafiq realized what he said and felt the need to explain.

'You know. Like a friend. Not like how a man loves a woman."

"Mmm hmm," Camilla laughed.

Minutes later, Rafiq pulled into the crowded Six Flags parking lot. After circling the lot, he pulled into an empty spot then killed the engine. He helped Camilla out of the truck before securing his car with the remote. They stood off to the side and waited for Boyce and Nakia who strolled up ten minutes later. After the men paid for the women, they headed inside and stood in line for the first rollercoaster they saw. Camilla tried to back out at the last minute but Rafiq convinced her that he had her. As the rollercoaster began to move, Camilla didn't even wait until they got to the top to start tripping. Rafiq laughed as she grabbed onto him for dear life burying her face in his chest. When the ride came to an end, Camilla had everyone in tears as she pushed her way through the crowd of people. She was making her way towards the exit but when Rafiq caught up with and calmed her down, he took her by the hand and they walked around the park trying to find something to do while Boyce and Nakia went on to the next roller coaster.

After Rafiq convinced Camilla to get on two more rides, they spent the rest of the afternoon playing games, winning prizes and eating food. When they decided to leave the park hours later, Rafiq was overwhelmed with joy as he saw the cheesy grin Camilla was sporting with her three giant stuffed animals in her hands. Placing her stuffed animals in the backseat, he helped her inside the truck, took his place behind the wheel and drove to their next destination which was Centennial park where the four of them posted up by the fountain watching the sunset as they talked about whatever came to mind. Rafiq was caught off guard when Camilla laid her head on his shoulder but that didn't stop him from placing his arm around her pulling her closer to him. As he basked in the moment, Rafiq knew that there was a strong vibe between them. He downplayed his feelings for Camilla when they were kids but he would be a fool if he made the same mistake twice.

When the sun was completely gone, and the stars were settled in the sky, the foursome decided to head home, but when Nakia pushed Boyce into the fountain of rings, an open stand-in water fountain for the public to play in. Rafiq picked Camilla up and carried her in as she screamed for him to stop. They ran through the fountain like kids as the girls tried to catch the boys. Chasing the boys back to the car, when the girls caught up to them, they jumped on their backs and they carried them the rest of the way. After Rafiq helped Camilla in the truck, he drove them back to his cousin's house and parked up. While they waited for Nakia and Boyce to return with their seafood platters, Rafiq used his key to let them in, they took their sneakers off leaving them at the front door.

"I can't believe your punk ass got me all wet," she laughed, "I should kill you." Camilla headed upstairs to the room she was sleeping in for the night.

"Kill the noise. You know you had fun today." He followed behind her.

"Yes. I did. I haven't had this much fun since we were kids," she flipped the switch for the lights. "Kane and I never did shit like this." She turned around to face him.

"Maybe we can shit like this more often." He licked his lips stepping her personal space.

"Rafiq I—"

Before she could finish her sentence, Rafiq forced his tongue down her throat roughly kissing her. Instead of kissing him back, Camilla pushed away from him.

"Rafiq, you know I'm still a married woman. I... we...shouldn't be doing this." She shook her head.

"Camilla, I loved ya ass since I was thirteen, and I know I downplayed my feelings for you back then but that was only because I was afraid to tell you how I felt. I thought you would reject me because I couldn't give you what you already had and feared you parents wouldn't approve of me but I don't give a fuck about none of that," he sincerely expressed, "I know your married and I know that shit is gonna take some time for you to get out of it and to get over that nigga but I wanna be ya man and if you give me a chance, I promise that I won't fuck it up."

As they stared at each other for a moment, Rafiq was having

a difficult time reading her. He wanted to believe that Camilla felt the same way as he did but if she didn't, he was going to feel like a fool.

"Rafiq, I've loved you since we were kids too," she softly responded, "I was too afraid to tell you because I saw the girls that you were into and even though I had money, I didn't carry myself the way they did," she chuckled, "But like I said earlier, I'm still finding my way and figuring some shit. I don't know how long it's gonna take for my divorce to be final or if he's even gonna sign the papers. All I know is that this shit is gonna be a process and I don't wanna start anything new or get you caught up in my bullshit."

"I was willing to fight for you before and I'm willing to do that now." He stepped closer to her." I'm not letting anyone keep me from you again. I love you Camilla and I'm gonna stand with you through it all."

Kissing her lips, Rafiq gripped her as she threw her arms around his neck. Their tongues danced wildly in each other's mouths as he removed her clothes tossing them to the floor. Removing his own clothes, Camilla's eyes grew wide at the sight of his long, thick shaft. Camilla climbed on the bed on all fours then Rafiq tongue kissed her pussy lips before sliding his dick inside making her moan.

"Fuuckk," he hissed as he began stroking her wetness.

Rafiq tightly gripped her hips as he fucked her at a medium pace. He tried not to go too deep because he didn't want to hurt her, and he was trying not to bust.

"Boy, if you don't stop playing and fuck this pussy," Camilla looked back at him.

Caught off guard by her words, he forcefully slammed his dick into her going as deep as he could. The moans and screams that escaped her mouth was like music to his ears as he pounded away at her pussy.

"Fuuckk! Oh my God!" She moaned throwing her ass back on his dick.

Going harder, Rafiq felt his nut building but when Camilla shouted that she was about to cum, he released his load inside of her, not caring about the consequences.

After they came down from their high, Rafiq threw on some dry clothes he had left at their crib while Camilla put on some dry clothes as well. Making their way downstairs, he posted up on the couch and flipped on the TV while she tossed their clothes in the dryer. When Camilla came back upstairs she sat next to him a few minutes before Boyce and Nakia walked in the door with their seafood meals in their hands. As the couple walked passed them, Rafiq and Camilla smirked at each other thinking that they were in clear but when Nakia announced that they heard them fucking, they couldn't do anything but laugh.

## 16

"No, no and for the last time no!" Maggie screamed as she followed her husband through the house. "We can't just let their marriage end because Kane made a mistake. This can be fixed, Richard."

"Look Maggie, I done already told you that I don't want my daughter anywhere near that motherfucker. I let that nigga mistreat and disrespect my daughter for the last time and I got a good mind to tell Camilla about his infidelity and his secret child," he angrily spoke putting on his suit jacket, "And from the conversation I had with her the other day, Camilla is heavily suggesting getting a divorce."

"A divorce!" she gasped, "Well did you try to talk her out of it?" Maggie stood in front of him.

"Now why the hell would I do something like that when I don't want them to be together, Maggie!"

"They can't get a divorce." She shook her head. "That's unacceptable."

"Why the hell are you so hellbent on them staying together?" Richard questioned in confusion. "This man has degraded and almost attacked our daughter. He cheated on her and had a baby outside their marriage. We wanted our daughter to have the best, and Kane done proved to us time and time again that he is far from that."

"I know that he may have a few anger issues and he's a bit controlling but these are issues that can be fixed with some counseling and anger management classes," she defended him, "I'm thinking about what's best for our daughter, Richard. You know Camilla is not capable of standing on her own two feet. She needs a wealthy man to take care of her and who better than the son of your best friend?"

"For your information, our daughter has always been capable of taking care of herself because we raised her to be independent until you decided that she needed to be taken care of! I shoulda spoke up when you presented me with the idea of having a twenty-two-year-old man marry our eighteen-year-old daughter! I let you manipulate, and mind fuck me for far too long Maggie and from now on, I'm going to have Camilla's best interest at heart! We can try to tell her what to do but at the end of the day, this is Camilla's marriage and she has the final say!" he shouted at her. "I don't know when you lose sight of your responsibilities as a mother but you need to get them the fuck back."

Walking around her, Maggie stood in the middle of their bedroom fuming with anger. She thought that fucking her husband's brains out that morning would cause him to give in to her like he always did over the years but since her ways were no longer working on Richard, she didn't know if she was losing her touch or if he was getting hip to her ways. As she began pacing the floor, her husband's words were ringing loudly in her head and although there were truth to his words, it was too late for Maggie to start doing the right thing after the mess she had made and she'd be damned if she got caught up because her brat of a daughter wanted to fuck up her plans.

When Camilla was old enough to start traveling around the

city on her own, Maggie was paranoid that something would happen to her while Richard remained calm and told her to let their daughter be. Ignoring her husband's advice, she hired a private investigator to follow her and her hood rat friends around. The private investigator reported to her and her only on a weekly basis but he never had nothing to report. They would get into a few fights around the neighborhood but most of the time they just chilled and roamed around. Maggie was about to fire the private investigator but when he showed her pictures of Camilla and one of the boys she was hanging with cuddled up together, she didn't care if their friendship was innocent like her daughter explained it to her, Maggie needed to put a stop to it before it became something more. She told the P.I to find out everything he could about the young thug and when she found out that he was into the streets, Maggie had everything she needed to blackmail him to leave Camilla alone. She offered him money, video games, new clothes and even a car on a few different occasions but he declined all of her offers. He was determined to remain in Camilla's life, but Maggie had other plans for him.

On a hot summer night, Camilla and her henchman spotted the young thug amongst a group of people on the corner. The henchman jumped out of the car, walked down the block and opened fired on the group. As the group scattered, the henchman chased a few of the boys while Maggie planted drugs in the young thug's backyard in his usual hiding spot. As soon as she made it back to her car, she called the cops and fabricated her story to get the young thug locked up. When her henchman confirmed that the young thug was locked up and was sentenced to life in prison for murder and the drugs they found, Maggie put her plan in motion for Camilla and Kane to be together.

She told Kane everything he needed to do to get her Camilla from her favorite things to her strong dislikes and once they got married, Maggie was confident that Kane was going to do right by Camilla but when she learned of his fuckery, she encouraged her daughter to stay because of all the foul shit she had done for them to be together. When she heard that the young thug, later known as Rafiq Sanders, was being released and that the henchman and the people he paid to lie for her turned themselves in, Maggie knew that it was only a matter of time before the truth would come out about her having him set up. If Camilla divorced Kane, all of her hard work would be for nothing and Maggie was not about to have that. She didn't care about his shortcomings or the fact that she got another bitch pregnant. They were going to stay together weather Camilla liked it or not.

Snatching up her purse and car keys, Maggie jumped in her champagne color 2019 Jaguar and drove to Kane's mansion. As she pulled into the driveway twenty minutes later, saw Kane walking inside with a baby in his arms. Killing the engine, Maggie hopped slamming the car door shut and jogged over to him.

"Miss Maggie, I don't mean no disrespect but I'm in no mood to talk. I just wanna spend time with my daughter and chill," Kane weariedly spoke.

"Boy, I don't give a damn what you in the mood for. Me and you have some things to discuss and I'm not leaving here until we do." She glared at him.

Taking a deep breath, Kane moved to the side and she marched inside.

"What do we need to talk about, Miss Maggie," he annoyingly sighed.

"Camilla, and how you're gonna get her back."

"As much as I would love to be back with Camilla, I'm not sure if she's gonna come back to me. She's doing her own thing now."

"What are you talking about?"

"The bakery she's working at is doing great, she moved out and she has people in her life that care about her. All the shit I bought for her, she returned. The car, clothes, phone and keys. I don't have a way of contacting her. I don't know where she lives, and I haven't seen or spoken to her since I got my ass whooped by her friends' husband." He made his way towards the living room with his daughter in his arms.

"That damn, Nakia." She followed behind him. "That girl always had a powerful influence over Camilla and not in so much of a negative way, but still." She shook her head. "Anyway, when did she move out?"

"Camilla has been gone for almost two months now." Kane placed his daughter on the floor before sitting on the couch. "I've been wanting to pop up at her job and plead my case to her, but now that Sheena is in town, I don't wanna be spotted with her or my daughter out in public."

"And what's her deal?" Maggie sat on the couch across from him.

"Sheena is basically blackmailing me. I have to take care of her, and if I don't, she's gonna tell Camilla and possibly the world about us." He rubbed his temples. "She had a good job and everything, but she quit just so she could live off me."

"I understand that you got a lot of shit going on right now, but I need for you to get out ya damn feelings and get back into the game because Camilla is talking about divorcing ya ass and I can't let that happen."

"Divorce? She really wants a divorce?" he asked surprisingly.

"Yes, and I went through too much in order for y'all to be together and I'm not about to let this marriage go down the drain," Maggie firmly stated. "Now, we have to get you and Camilla in the same room together. So that means you're gonna have to call Richard and set up a meeting with him because I got a feeling that Camilla is not gonna meet with you unless her father is there."

"So now I gotta have supervised visits with my wife?"

"Well if you wouldn't have tried to attack her and did right by her that first time, you wouldn't be in this mess. I swear I would kill you myself for the bullshit you put my daughter through but being as though I believe that you can change for the better, I'm willing to help."

"Okay," he sighed. "So I gotta set up a meeting with Richard and what else?"

"Find a good marriage counselor and sign up for anger management classes. It'll show that you're taking steps towards changing and send her gifts like flowers and stuff to her job. Get in touch with your romantic side. Hell, google some shit. Just do what you need to do to get back in her good graces." She stood to her feet to leave.

"I'll start working on that now." He rose to his feet walking her to the door. "I appreciate you helping me, Miss Maggie. I won't let you down this time."

"You better not you lil son of a bitch, because if Camilla comes back to you and you hurt her in any way, shape or form, I'm gonna kill you, that bitch Sheena, and your illegitimate child in there," Maggie warned. "Don't make me look bad, Kane."

Heading back to her car with a smile on her face, she hopped behind the wheel of her car and headed home. Pulling in her driveway, her phone began to ring parked her car in the middle of the driveway to answer it.

"Well if it isn't my favorite private investigator. How are you doing, Kenny?"

"I'm doing well, Maggie. It's been a long time."

"Yes it has. Too long, but I need some info on a few folks and need your help."

"A few folks? Define a few."

"Six people total."

"Damn, Maggie," he chuckled. "You do know I'm only one person. I can't investigate six people at once. Plus, I'm working on a very big case now that I'm dedicated to but since I like you. I'll see what I can do."

"Thanks, Kenny."

Ending the call, Maggie parked her car in her usual spot making her way inside her home. A satisfying feeling had taken over her body as she put another plan in motion. To make sure that Camilla would definitely go back to Kane, she needed to take away her circle of positivity, and although she wasn't sure if Rafiq crossed paths with Camilla yet, she needed to get to him before he did. Anyone that was team Camilla and that was encouraging her to move on with her life needed to go. She wanted her daughter in the same state she was in before she linked back up Nakia. She was determined to see her plan through, and whoever stood in her way was going to be laid to rest. Including her husband.

## 17

As Camilla bounced through the bakery with a smile on her face, she had never recalled feeling this good or being this happy in her life. Since she separated from Kane with the help of her dad, Camilla woke up every morning with a smile on her face and so did her son. She felt like she had a reason to get out of bed in the morning for something other than just feeding her son, shopping, cleaning and exercising. Camilla never expected her life to turn around as quickly as it did, but she was grateful for the booming business, her friends, father, and the constant positive vibes. With each passing day, the love she had for Kane was slowly fading and her thoughts of making their marriage work were fading as well. With thoughts of Rafiq occupying her mind throughout her day, the only thing that would be left of Kane were memories.

After giving the customer her change for the two dozen cupcakes she ordered, Camilla went to the back to check on the brownies that were baking while Nakia continued to mop the floor. Inspecting the brownies like she had been trained to do, she placed the tray back in the oven to let them bake a few more minutes. Removing her oven mitts, Camilla grabbed two trays of the freshly baked oatmeal and chocolate chip cookies carrying them to the front of the store, placing them in the glass display case.

"Damn. It's only one in the afternoon and we're almost sold out of everything." Nakia placed the mop in the bucket. "The only thing we have is cake, and even that is almost gone."

"That commercial really helped you with your business. I didn't think business would pick up damn near overnight," Camilla stated.

"That's because the wife of the 2018 and 19 businessmen of the year endorsed my bakery," she playfully nudged her, "I can't thank you enough for helping me out the way you did, C."

"Girl don't even mention it," she smiled, "Besides, it's the least I could do. Reconnecting with you literally changed my life and I can't thank you enough for the encouragement and confidence you've given me."

"I'm not gonna lie. When I first ran back into you and you told us how you were living, I wanted to cuss you out so bad because you were letting that man control every inch of your life and that was not the Camilla I knew. All I did was open your eyes to the fact that it was more to life but it was you who actually took the first step to start living it and I'm so proud of you," Nakia smiled at her.

"Thanks sis." She gave her bestie a quick hug.

The sound of the bell ringing on the door caught their attention. When the ladies saw the large bouquet of roses and the 'I'm Sorry' balloons that the delivery man was carrying, they looked at each other with confusion. When the delivery man told them that he had a delivery for Camilla Jacobs, she signed for the package and removed the vase from his hands.

"Why the hell is Rafiq sending you I'm sorry balloons? What the fuck did he do?"

"They're not from Rafiq Kia. They're from Kane." Camilla stared at the card with his name on it.

"Dear Camilla, there's not a day that goes by that you don't cross my mind. I'm missing you like crazy and I feel like I'm losing my mind. I know I fucked up but I think we can fix this. Please reach out to me soon. I love you, Kane." Camilla read the note aloud.

"You shoulda known that nigga was gonna try to get you back sooner or later, C. Now that you have proved that you don't need him and you're doing well on your own, he feels that you're slipping away and wants to work on fixing your marriage before you serve his ass with them papers."

"You think that's really why he sent this? Because he feels like I'm slipping away from him?"

"Hell yeah!" she shouted. "The last time you seen that nigga, he tried to pounce on ya ass and got the snot beat outta him. You sent back all the shit he bought and moved the fuck out and now that you're moving on with your life, he's starting to miss ya ass. The question is why is he starting to miss you? Is it out of love or guilt? Is there a motive behind these gifts? Is this really him sending these gifts or someone sending them for him?" Nakia seriously stated.

"You got a point there Kia. All of the gifts he'd given me were all for a reason which I never found out." she nodded her. "And there could be another motive behind this shit besides him missing me, but I don't know if I wanna take a chance on finding out."

"Do you still have feelings for Kane, C?"

"I do but since I've been messing around with Rafiq, I haven't given Kane much thought. I told Rafiq that it was gonna take me some time to figure out what I wanted to do as far as my life and marriage and he said that he's willing to wait for me. I just wanna make sure I'm done with Kane for sure before

I start something new with Rafiq," she sincerely stated, "The last thing I wanna do is hurt that man."

"You know I can't stand ya husband, but I do think you have a point. If you do decide to work on your marriage, just don't let him turn you back into the Camilla he's used to. I'll go crazy if someone tries to keep us apart again."

"So will I."

Carrying the vase of flowers and balloons to the back of the store, Camilla reread the card once more before returning to the front of the store. As customers flooded the store, she found it hard to concentrate with thoughts of Kane and Rafiq flooding her mind. For the past few weeks, Rafiq had been giving Camilla some of the best dick she ever had in her life and she couldn't get enough of the time they shared together. Whether they were chilling at his crib watching movies or having date night at an expensive restaurant, Camilla enjoyed just being around him. Unlike Kane, Rafiq didn't have a problem with Camilla living her life and chasing her dreams. He was hype when she informed him that she would be attending Spelman College in the fall and was proud of her for doing something she always wanted to do. His encouragement, support and wise advice was endless and even though they wanted to be together, Camilla never stopped viewing him as her friend. The type of relationship she was building with Rafiq was something she thought she had with Kane but Camilla learned that she was wrong. Hands down, she knew she should be with Rafiq but something inside of her was pulling her towards Kane.

After dealing with dozens of customers, the ladies were worn out when closing time approached. As the last customer walked out of the store, a brown skin thick chick with long Brazilian weave walked in. When the women noticed the designers she was rocking along with the Burberry briefcase in her hand, they knew they were dealing with a woman with some money.

"Hello ma'am," Camilla greeted with a smile. "Welcome to Nakia's Sweet Treats. How may I help you?"

"Hello Camilla," the woman responded smugly, "I've been dying to meet you."

"Do I know you?" she asked confused.

"No but me and you have a lot in common."

"How the fuck so?" Nakia rolled her neck stepping from behind the counter with Camilla behind her.

"I understand that you are the wife of Kane Jacobs. Is that correct?"

"Yeah." Camilla stepped from behind her friend.

"Well I just wanted to inform you honey, that your husband had an affair a year or so ago and from that affair, a child was born." The woman smirked.

"What the fuck!" Nakia shouted.

"No. No. That can't be true." Camilla shook her head in disbelief.

"Oh but I'm afraid it is." The woman reached into her briefcase removing a document. "Here is the paternity test results for his nearly two year old daughter." She handed the paper to Camilla.

As her eyes carefully scanned the paper, Camilla's heart damn near stopped when she saw that Kane was indeed the father of a little girl.

"This shit is false." Nakia shouted. "Who gave this shit to you? Who the fuck are you?"

"I'm Sheena. The mother of his daughter, Kaylynn and this is far from false. Kane is my daughter's father."

"When the fuck did he have time to have an affair? Kane is always working. Camilla snapped.

"Yeah. He was working aight," Sheena chuckled, "But not the type of work you're thinking about."

Lunging towards her, Camilla swung on the bitch but missed due to Nakia holding her back.

"Let me the fuck go, Nakia!" she fought to break free.

"No need to get physical, honey. I came here to let you know that your husband has another child in the world and before you start thinking that I just ignored the fact that he was married, I didn't. I was unaware that he was married until I saw your commercial and you said who you were. Hell, I didn't even know he was as wealthy as he is until I looked him up. So, I can't be blamed for not knowing, but I will say this. Me and my child have been a secret for too long and we will not be a secret any longer. I want my child to be acknowledged and accepted by everyone in Kane's life. Including you, Camilla. We're family whether you like it or not. So, get the fuck use to it because we're not going anywhere." Sheena switched out of the bakery

"Fuck you bitch!" Camilla screamed at her.

She tried to run after her but Nakia blocked her path.

"Camilla you gotta calm down!" She placed her hands on her shoulders. "I know you're pissed off right now but instead of taking your frustration out on shawty, direct that anger towards your damn husband!"

Letting her besties words sink in, Camilla took a few deep breaths to calm herself down.

"You good now, sis?"

"Yeah," she nodded her head. "Are we finished here? I need to go. I gotta talk to my dad."

"Yeah. Go ahead. I can lock up. Just call me when you get in so I can know your cool."

"Okay."

"Oh and I put something in the trunk of your car. Just a little thank you gift for helping me out with my business." Nakia winked at her.

Giving her friend a small smile, Camilla snatched up her things and headed out the door. Popping the locks to her car, she jumped behind the wheel placing her things in the passenger seat. Removing her phone from her purse, she called her dad asking where he was and when he told her that he was at her father-in laws house, Camilla told him that she was in route before starting her car and pulling into traffic

As she drove to Karl's house, she couldn't fight the tears that were pouring from her eyes. Kane's controlling ways and mistreatment was hard enough to deal with but learning that he had an affair and a baby on her was a tough pill to swallow. Why would he put her through so much heartache and pain when she was nothing but a good woman and wife to him. Despite the way he treated her, Camilla remained loyal to him and she trusted him with every ounce of her being and for him to do this to her was the ultimate disrespect. The thoughts that she had of them fixing their marriage were completely gone. There was only so much a woman could take and learning about his baby mama was the final straw.

# 18

---

When Richard heard how upset his daughter was, he knew something was wrong. He just didn't know what. He knew it had to be something big because instead of waiting until he got home so they could talk privately, Camilla decided to come to Karl's which meant that she needed to talk to him asap. Tucking his phone in his pocket, Richard stepped back inside Karl's office picking his drink up from the desk.

"Is everything okay?" Karl inquired.

"That was Camilla. She needs to talk to me about something. So, she'll be here soon."

"It must be something important if she's meeting you here."

"Yeah I know. I guess we'll find out what it is when she gets here." Richard took a swig of his drink.

"Look Richard, I know that things haven't been the same between us since Camilla separated from Kane and I just want to apologize for the role I played in it." He leaned on his desk. "I knew from the jump that Kane wasn't ready for marriage but because I wanted to believe in him, I convinced you and

Maggie that he was the right choice for your daughter and I truly regret my decision to do so."

"I appreciate the apology old friend but it wasn't just you who played a part in this mess. It was my fault as well." he sat down in one of the office chairs.

"What do you mean?"

"I had my doubts about the two of them getting married, but I let Maggie persuade me into thinking that this was the right thing to do," he chuckled, "But now I realized that it was all a part of her plan."

"What plan? What's going on with Maggie?"

"A couple of days ago, a detective friend of mine called me to his office to discuss an old case that has been reopened and when he told me that my wife's name was at the center of their investigation, it took everything in me to keep my composure. He told me that a young man was falsely accused of murdering three people and dealing cocaine nearly seven years ago and when his case was reopened, the people involved turned themselves in and they claim the person behind this scheme is Maggie."

"Are you fucking serious!" he gasped in shock.

"As a heart attack." He downed the rest of his drink.

"Why the hell would Maggie do some shit like that? It doesn't make any sense."

Before he could respond, the front door buzzed, and Karl let Camilla in.

"We'll finish talking about this when she leaves," Richard whispered before his daughter stormed in with a piece of paper in her hands.

"I wanna divorce!" she shouted with tears streaming down her face.

"What?" the men asked in unison.

"I want a fucking divorce! I will not be married to Kane's ass a minute longer! So, call a lawyer so we can get this process started!" Camilla huffed.

"Babygirl, calm down," Richard softly spoke pulling her in for a hug.

"Why? Why would he do this to me dad?" she sobbed.

"Do what Camilla? What did Kane do?"

"He had a fucking baby on me!" she broke out of his embrace holding up the paper. "Some bitch named Sheena came into the bakery telling me how me and her have kids by the same man! This is the paternity results!" Camilla handed her father the paper.

He read the results and the paper confirmed what he already knew. Richard passed the paper to Karl who read the result as well before placing the paper on his desk.

"Did you know about this Karl?" she stepped closer to his desk.

He shifted his eyes to the floor.

"You knew about your son's affair and you didn't tell me?" Camilla cried even harder.

"Daughter-in-law, I wanted to tell you when I found out a few months but Kane told me to stay out of his marriage and I had to respect his wishes, but Kane wasn't the one who told me. Sheena's father is a friend of mine and he told me about them." Karl handed her his phone.

Richard's heart broke as he watched his daughter stare at the picture of Kane and his other family.

"So, all the business trips he went on to North Carolina and Philly, he was spending time with them?"

"He was only lying about the trips to North Carolina. We don't have anything out there," Karl sadly replied.

"That lying motherfucker!" she screamed, "I don't wanna work on my marriage anymore, dad. I don't wanna go to counseling or none of that shit. I wanna divorce."

"Are you sure Camilla? You're very upset right now. Don't you want to take a minute to calm down first, so you can think about this with a clear head?" Richard suggested.

"Am I thinking about this with a clear head dad. I want a divorce," Camilla clapped her hands together, "I don't wanna take this shit to court and I don't want to get lawyers involved. I just want us to have a meeting discussing the terms, sign the papers and get this shit over with. I don't want this shit to be dragged out."

"Okay baby girl," Richard nodded his head. I'll get my lawyer to draw up the divorce papers and once I have them, I'll set up a meeting at my house inviting all the parties involved and I'll act as a witness on your behalf."

"Thanks dad." She kissed his cheek.

"Camilla, from the bottom of my heart, I'm so sorry that my son put you through all of this." Karl stood to his feet.

"I am too." Camilla dried her eyes. "I'll see y'all later."

Once Camilla was gone, Richard grabbed the bottle of Gin from the shelf pouring himself and Karl a drink. The two men took huge gulps from their glasses before sitting back in their chairs.

"I can't believe that girl showed up at Camilla's job." Karl stated in disbelief.

"This situation just keeps getting uglier and uglier. I'm happy that Camilla wants a divorce, but the truth of the matter is Kane is not gonna give her up without a fight." Richard shook his head.

"This is true," Karl sighed, "I don't know if he really loves Camilla or if it's his pride but whatever it is, he's holding onto that girl for some reason."

The room fell silent for a moment as they took another swig of alcohol.

"So, what are you gonna do about Maggie? You know she's gonna lie if you ask her anything about this."

"I'm gonna have to do some investigating of my own. Maggie and I haven't seen eye to eye on things in the past two years. Since I stopped being pussy whipped and started seeing her for the bitch she truly is, I'm thinking about getting a divorce my damn self." He seriously stated.

As he finished the rest of his drink, Richard and Karl had a brief discussion about business before he gave his friend a handshake and left. Instead of heading home to his mansion, Richard drove to one of his luxury condos in downtown Atlanta. That was one of the many properties he had that his wife didn't know about. When he arrived at his condo, Richard sat down on the couch removing his ringing phone from his pocket and answering it.

"Aye, Kenny. What you got for me?"

"Hey, Rich. I was just calling to let you know that Maggie called me the other day. She said that she has six people she wants me to investigate."

"Did she give you names?"

"Nah. I told her that I was working on a big case at the moment and wasn't sure if I was gonna be able to dedicate my time to hers. I never told her I was working for you."

"Good. Good." He nodded his head. "Well since she wants six people to be investigated, do you think she might want the young man she was spying on years ago investigated now that he's out of prison?"

"She might."

"How do you feel about doing double duty?"

"I don't mind if the price is right."

"Cool. Here's what I want you to do."

Richard instructed that Kenny keep an eye on Maggie and whoever she wanted him to investigate and whatever he found out, Kenny was to report to him first before he gave any information to Maggie. After they agreed on the price, Richard ended the call, kicking his feet up on his table while sporting a devious grin. As much as he didn't want to believe that his wife was up to no good, he couldn't deny the change in her over the years. Richard had been a fool for Maggie for far too long, and he refused to be a fool any longer.

## 19

Waking up early Friday morning, Rafiq felt like he was on top of the world. With his cousins' garage coming along and Camilla in his life, he felt like he had everything. Rafiq had been helping his cousin get his auto shop off the ground since he was released from prison. Boyce had a thing for customizing car and helping people make their dream cars a reality. So, when he asked Rafiq to be a part of his lifelong dream, he couldn't refuse. Although he didn't know the first thing about fixing cars, Rafiq was willing to go to trade school to learn how to be an automotive engineer which would add to the technology degree he obtained in prison. Once Boyce's auto shop was open, he was going to let Rafiq do his hands-on training there as he went to school. The fact that he had to go back to school didn't sit right with him, but he wasn't just doing it for himself, he was also doing it for his aunt Jackie. There wasn't a day that passed that he didn't think about her and the pain from her death still consumed his soul. There were times when he wanted to return to the streets making fast money like he used to, but that would be a huge slap in the face to his aunt and cousin who had done so much to get him out of prison and they wanted him to stay on the straight and narrow and with the fifty grand that his Aunt Jackie left for him, that was more than enough motivation to keep him out of the streets

As his career was headed in the positive direction, Rafiq believed that his love life was heading in a positive direction as well. Since their day of fun at Six Flags, he had fallen head over for Camilla and he couldn't get enough of her. She was the bright spot of his day and even though he had told himself that he was going to give her space as she figured things out with her marriage and life goal, Rafiq couldn't stay away from her. If they weren't cuddled up on the couch together, they were having a long discussion on the phone. Camilla was the missing piece that he needed to complete him, and he wasn't about to let her go.

After making his bed, Rafiq hopped in the shower and got dressed in a black Dickie jumpsuit which was his work clothes. As he laced up his Timbs, his phone began to ring on his night-stand. Knowing it was Camilla calling from the tone, he answered with a smile.

"Wassup, beautiful. How are you doing this morning?"

"Not good," she sniffled.

"Camilla what's wrong? Why are you crying?" His smiled quickly faded.

"Yesterday, I found out my...husband had an affair...and had a baby on me," she sobbed.

"Say what?"

"My husband's baby mama marched into my job and told me and Nakia that my husband is the father of her one-year old daughter. She had the paternity test results and everything."

"That bitch could be lying Camilla." He tried to defend the bastard.

"No, she's not," she choked out, "My father-in-law showed me a picture of my husband, his baby mama and their daughter and that child looks like my son. This shit is real Rafiq. I wanted to believe that bitch was lying too but she wasn't. I tried not to let this shit bother me but I've been crying all night about this shit."

"Damn, Camilla," he sighed, "I'm sorry that you're going this shit. You didn't deserve any of the shit that nigga put you through and I know your hurting right now but believe me when I tell you that you're gonna get through this. Aight?"

"Thanks, Rafiq. I needed to hear that. I just dropped Kannon off at summer camp and I told Nakia that I wouldn't be coming to work today. So I'm just gonna be in the crib getting my mind right for this meeting I'm gonna have with my husband."

"What meeting is that?"

"To sign the divorce papers," she replied confidently, "After ole girl told me about their affair and their child, that was the final straw. I let that nigga disrespect me for too long and now his ass gots ta go."

"Are you sure about that?"

"I'm absolutely positive. There is no fixing this shit. I'm done with his ass," Camilla stated sternly, "Well I just wanted to call and let you know what was going on. So, if I don't answer my phone, don't take it personal. I'm just taking some time to myself."

"It's cool Camilla. Take all the time you need. You know I ain't going nowhere."

"Talk to you later."

When the line went dead, Rafiq started to do the James Brown. Hearing that Camilla was finally going to get a divorce from her punk ass husband was music to his ears. For the past month, he was unsure if she was going to go back to her husband or not and as badly as he wanted to know, Rafiq never asked Camilla about it. He wanted to spend their time together enjoying each other. Not talking about all the fucked things her husband did but now that he had the answer to the question that was burning a hole in his brain, Rafiq could breathe easy knowing that he was next in line to be with the woman he loved.

Stuffing his phone and a couple of racks in his pocket, he grabbed his keys and headed out the door. Rafiq popped the locks to his truck, jumped behind the wheel and brought it to life. Before he put the car in drive, his phone played a tone indicating he had a text. Removing his phone from his pocket, he read the message from his cousin telling him to get to his house a.s.a.p. Quickly placing the phone back in his pocket, Rafiq pulled out of the lot driving like a speed demon to his cousins' house. Coming to a screeching halt minutes later, he killed the engine, jumped his car and dashed inside the house. Boyce was standing behind the couch with his arm around Nakia as two gentlemen, a black man and a white man, stood to their feet to greet him

"Good morning, Mr. Sanders. My name is Detective Jackson, and this is my partner Detective Lewis. We would like to ask you a few questions...in private."

"I don't mind answering your questions but my family stays," Rafiq sternly stated.

"Are you sure, Mr. Sanders?"

"Yeah." He walked over to the sofa and sat down.

Nakia and Boyce joined him on the couch while the detectives sat across from them.

"Mr. Sanders, We understand that you were recently released because the crimes you were convicted for were false," Detective Lewis spoke, "The suspects that were involved in framing you have turned themselves in and are now serving life sentences."

"I'm aware of that," Rafiq nodded his head.

"The men who turned themselves in said that it was a

female that was the mastermind behind the scheme to frame you," Detective Jackson added, "Do you know this woman?"

The detective removed a picture from his inside coat pocket and he cringed at the sight of Camilla's mom, Maggie.

"Yes I do. That's Maggie Hayes. She's the mother of a friend of ours." He glared at the picture.

"Are you referring to Camilla Hayes-Jacobs?"

"Yeah."

"And when did you first meet Maggie Hayes, Mr. Sanders?" Detective Jackson put the photo back in his coat.

"I first met Maggie a few weeks before my seventeenth birthday. She approached me when I was on my way home from school. She tried to bribe me to stay away from Camilla because she didn't want her daughter hanging out with a dude like me. Maggie offered me money, a car, video games and clothes on a few separate occasions, but I declined her offers."

"You never told me that," Boyce spoke out in shock.

"I didn't tell anybody. Rafiq looked in his cousin's direction. "I thought that she would be impressed with the fact that I didn't scare easily, and I wanted her to know that there was nothing she could offer me to make me leave Camilla alone."

"So, you mean to tell me that Maggie Hayes went through the trouble of setting you up to keep you away from her daughter?" Detective Lewis asked in disbelief.

"Like I told you. She didn't want Camilla hanging out with me," Rafiq reiterated.

"Okay." Detective Lewis nodded his head. "Did Maggie Hayes know your aunt?"

"I don't think so." He looked at them with confusion. "What does my aunt have to do with this?"

"Well, Mr. Sanders, we're not sure but we believe Maggie Hayes may be the prime suspect in your aunt's murder."

"What!" The three of them shouted in unison.

"Like I said, we're not sure but the police camera's that are on your aunt's street caught footage of her car driving down the block but we can't see her going in or coming out of the house. Like I said, Maggie Hayes is a prime suspect in this investigation, but we don't have any concrete evidence to obtain her but believe me when I tell you that we're working hard on this case and we'll let you know if we get any new information."

The detectives rose to their feet to leave. Rafiq walked them to the door shaking their hands on their way out the door.

"I can't believe this shit." Nakia jumped up from the couch. "That bitch done framed my cousin and possibly killed my mother in law! That bitch gotta fucking go! I never liked that bitch! It's one thing to fuck with and talk about me but when you fuck with my family, that's when shit gets serious!" she paced the floor.

"I agree." Boyce stood to his feet. "I love Camilla like a sister and I consider her to be family, but her mom's is outta pocket. She done did some fucked up shit and killed mama to cover her fucking tracks. That bitch can't live after this shit."

"I hear what y'all saying and believe me I want Maggie's head hanging on my fucking wall somewhere, but we can't do this shit ourselves even though I would like for us too. I just don't want neither of us sitting behind bars for killing this bitch. We got too much to live for." Rafiq stated.

"You're right about that," Nakia chimed in, "Damn. I just can't believe that bitch is this spiteful. She didn't even take the time to get to know you. She just judged a book by the cover and assumed that you were no good for Camilla. Yeah, you were in the streets but you're a better man than the piece of shit that her daughter is married to."

"It is what it is cuz. We can't turn back the hands of time. The only question running through my mind is do we tell Camilla about this or just keep it between us?" Rafiq asked.

"I think she needs to know what the fuck her mama did. I don't think we should tell her right now because of all the shit she got going on right now but once she gets a better handle on the situation with her husband, we should sit her down and tell her together," Nakia suggested.

The men nodded their head in agreement.

"What the hell do we do until then? Because this shit is gonna be hard to put on the back burner." Boyce asked.

"We go on with our lives. I'm sure Maggie knows that I'm outta jail now. So, I got a feeling that she's gonna be paying me a visit soon and since she's killing people to cover her tracks. She might try to kill me too and if Maggie wants to go that route, then so be it but I know for a fact that I'm gonna be the last one standing."

## 20

After two months, three weeks and two days of not hearing his wife's voice, Kane damn near leaped for joy when Camilla called him from her fathers' phone telling him to meet her at her parents' house. He had been sending gifts to her for the past couple of weeks and he believed that the diamond tennis bracelet he had delivered two days prior lead to the phone he received that day. When the call ended, Kane quickly hopped in the shower, threw on one of his suits along with his jewelry, snatched up his keys, wallet and phone then dashed out of the house. Unlocking the doors to his truck, Kane jumped inside starting the car. As he pulled out of the driveway, his phone began to ring, but when he saw that it was Sheen, he declined the call. Kane was in too good of a mood to deal with her money-hungry ass and decided that he would deal with her after his meeting. Driving down the expressway, Kane was prepared to plead his case to Camilla. He couldn't wait to tell her how he had been attending anger management classes and that he had a marriage counselor on standby. Although Kane wasn't big on going to his weekly anger management courses, he was willing to do whatever it took to get his woman back.

Pulling into the driveway of his in-laws' house, Kane was surprised to see his father's car parked on the other side. He found it strange that he didn't see Maggie's car there, but he really didn't want to see her anyway. After the threat she made to kill him, Sheena and Kaylynn, Kane needed to focus on the task at hand to prevent her from making good on her threat. Parking next to his fathers' car, he jumped out of his car strolling to the front door. Ringing the doorbell, a husky man in a black suit answered the door. Kane gave the guard his name and he let him pass instructing him to go down the hall. When he entered the office, he locked eyes with Camilla whose face was like stone and so was Richard's. Karl was standing behind an empty chair that he assumed was for him and a table was between the chairs.

"Glad you could make it, Kane. Come in and have a seat." Richard pointed to the chair.

Making his way over to the empty seat, Kane sat down keeping his eyes focused on Camilla. She looked beautiful in her navy-blue pants suit. Her curly hair cascaded around her face and it seemed like her brown eyes were looking deep into his soul.

"I just want to point out that this meeting is between Kane and Camilla," Karl stated, "Richard and I are here to make sure this meeting goes smoothly and to act as witnesses on behalf of our children."

"Who wants to start first?" Richard asked.

"I do," Kane answered quickly.

"Okay, Kane. You have the floor. Camilla, you are not to interrupt him while he is talking." Richard tapped her shoulder and she nodded her head.

"Camilla, I know that I haven't been the best man and

husband to you. I stripped away all of the things that attracted me to you in the beginning because I didn't know how to handle a strong, opinionated woman who knew her worth. I was intimidated by your strength and the way people gravitated towards you and I feared that if I let you be all you could that you would find somebody better than me," he paused, "I know I can't make up for the years where I treated you like a prisoner but I would like for us to start over again. I'm going to anger management classes now and I found a counselor who's waiting for us to set up our first appointment. I wanna do things right this time, Camilla, if you agree to let me."

The room fell silent for a moment as Kane kept his eyes locked on Camilla as he waited for her to speak.

"Is that all you have to say?"

"Yes."

"Very well." She sat up straight in her chair. "I didn't call you hear so we could discuss fixing our marriage. I called you hear so we could discuss the terms of our divorce, Kane." Camilla removed the divorce documents from her briefcase along with a pen, placing them on the table.

"Divorce?"

"That's right. Over the past two and a half months we've been separated, I thought about us fixing our marriage because despite the way you treated me, I believed that we could work through our problems and move forward. But when a woman named Sheena came to my job and told me about your affair and one-year old daughter, that was the final straw," she sternly stated, "And before you try to deny it, here are the paternity test results and a photo of y'all together." Camilla held the test results and the picture up then placed them on the table. "I was a good woman and wife to you, Kane, and all you did was mistreat, lie, disrespect, and betray me and I refuse to be married to you any longer."

Kane's expression went from calm to angry in a matter of

seconds as he stared at the photo of him, Kaylynn and Sheena and the paternity results. He couldn't believe that Sheena went behind his back and told Camilla about their child instead of keeping her word to him. Kane was backed into a corner with no way out. He knew the smart thing for him to do was to sign the papers and move on, but his pride wouldn't let him.

"So, if you agree to sign these papers now, we'll discuss how we're gonna split custody for Kannon, alimony and things of that nature. I'll sign the papers first."

Kane watched as Camilla signed her name on the line, slamming the pen down when she was finished. She slid the papers in his direction, waiting for him to do the same.

"I'm not signing shit," Kane stated sternly.

"Excuse me?"

"You heard me. I understand why you want a divorce and I don't blame, but you could at least give me a chance to redeem myself, Camilla."

"Redeem yourself? It's impossible for you to redeem yourself because once the trust is gone, so is the relationship Kane, and I don't trust you anymore. You don't have to sign these papers if you don't want to, but you're gonna give me my divorce one way or another."

"We'll see about that." Kane stood to his feet and left.

Power walking to his car, he jumped inside as his phone rang in the cupholder. Noticing that it was Sheena calling, Kane answered.

"Bitch I should kill ya ass!"

"Now is that anyway to talk to the mother of your child? Do you talk to Camilla that way?"

"Sheena, what the fuck were you thinking telling my wife about us? I've been taking care of ya ass since you got here. I held up my end of the bargain! Why didn't you hold up yours?" He roared speeding out of the driveway.

"Because Kane, I figured your wife had the right to know

about us and our daughter because I knew you were gonna continue to keep us a secret," she answered, "I told Camilla that I wanted our daughter to be accepted by everyone in your family, but now, I think I want to tell the world about us."

"Sheena, you can't do that. That shit will ruin my reputation, and that's public humiliation for my wife."

"You shoulda thought about that before you deceived me into thinking that you were single. I used to sit and drive myself crazy trying to figure out why the fuck you didn't want me. I was even thinking about getting cosmetic surgery to make myself more appealing, but when I saw your perfect, beautiful wife on TV, I understood why you couldn't be with me because you were committed to someone else! I loved you, Kane, and I was hoping that we could be a family but the time for that is over! I said I wanted the life that your wife had, and now, I'm about to have it all," Sheena snickered.

"What the fuck is that supposed to mean?"

"You'll see soon enough."

Placing his phone back in the cupholder, Kane began counting backwards from one hundred to calm himself down. What started out to be the happiest day of his life quickly turned into the worse. As he got closer to his mansion, his urge to squeeze the life from Sheena's body was growing stronger and stronger. If it wasn't for the stunt that she pulled with Camilla, he would have his wife back by now. Instead, he was going to have to plot, plan, scheme and revert to his old ways to get Camilla back and he was ready and willing to do anything.

As he pulled into the driveway of his home, Kane slammed on his breaks to prevent himself from hitting the crowd of people. When they turned around and saw him, the mob of people surrounded his car as the cameras began to flash. Noticing that the mob of people were reporters and cameraman, Kane became enraged with anger as he listened to the reporters shout questions at him about Sheena Walters. Gripping his steering wheel tightly, a million and one thoughts crossed his mind of how he was going to handle his baby mama for causing him to lose his wife and destroying his reputation. Kane knew that killing Sheena was a bit extreme but since she did the extreme, he had no choice but to do the same.

## 21

Maggie watched the news the following morning with her blood pressure through the roof. She listened to reporter talk about an anonymous tip that was received a couple of days about Kane Jacobs having an affair with a woman named Sheena Walters and he fathered a one-year old daughter outside of his marriage with Camilla Jacobs. She couldn't believe that someone went to the public about his infidelity and she knew that it would only be a matter of time before Camilla saw it, if she hadn't seen it already.

"Can you believe this shit, Richard." Maggie turned the tv off with the remote. "Who the fuck leaked the story about Kane and his bastard child?"

"I don't know Maggie, but this story is everywhere." He held up the newspaper he was reading. "I'll call Camilla and see how she's dealing with this. I can't imagine how she's feeling." He slid his feet into his slippers. "This type of public humiliation will work in our favor when we go to court in a couple of weeks."

"Go to court for what?"

"To see a judge about their divorce."

"She's still going through with this?"

"Yes, Maggie," he sighed, "Camilla and Kane had a meeting a couple of days ago to sign the divorce papers without going through the trouble of lawyers and Kane refused to sign. So we're going to court.

"What! Why the hell wouldn't you tell me about the meeting Richard?" She jumped out of bed.

"For what Maggie? So, you can sit there and try to manipulate Camilla into seeing things your way like you used to do? You were better off not being there." Richard headed towards the door.

"I was only doing what I thought was best for Camilla and regardless of what I think she should do, I still needed to be there. I'm her mother for Christ's sake and your wife. You shouldn't be keeping things from me, Richard."

Richard stopped in his tracks turning around to face her.

"It's strange for you to say that Maggie since you've been keeping shit from me for years." He glared at her.

"I..I... I don't know what you're talking about," she stuttered with wide eyes.

"You're a terrible liar, Maggie. You've always been, but I was too stupid and too trusting to think that you could do no wrong," he chuckled, "But now, I'm starting to see you for the conniving and manipulative bitch you really are."

"Wh..Wha...What! Richard why are you talking to me like this? What has gotten into you?"

"Some damn sense Maggie. That's what have gotten into me!" He roared. "Before I found out all the shit that you were telling Camilla to deal with, I felt like something was off between us for nearly three years now and I've been trying to figure out why that is but I think I finally have the answer."

"And what's that?"

"Let me put it like this. If I find out that there is any truth to the shit I've been hearing about you, Camilla won't be the only one getting a divorce." He glared at her before leaving the room.

Frozen in place, Maggie's heart rate rapidly increased causing her to become numb with fear. Her head began to spin as she thought about all the possible things her husband could've possibly heard about her and none of it was good. The twenty years that she had been married to Richard, Maggie did her best to maintain an upstanding reputation as the wife of boss and to the outside world, she was that indeed but to the men and women who prevented her from getting her way or got in the way of her plans, they saw the dangerous side of her that she kept concealed from Richard. She was always the type of woman that got what she wanted, no matter if it was by choice or force. Maggie was aware of her violent and conniving ways since she was a child and although she did her best to keep them at bay, she couldn't contain herself when issues would occur. Whenever Maggie saw a problem or felt that there would be one, she took it upon herself to handle it without finding out the facts first. Her jumping to conclusions got her in more trouble than none and being as though she did the same thing with Rafiq, her evil and vindictive ways had come back to bite her in the ass.

With her ringing phone snapping her out of her thoughts, Maggie tossed the cover back in search for her phone. When she found it, she declined the call and headed to the bathroom where she washed up and got dressed for the day. In desperate need to talk to her daughter, she tossed her phone in her purse, snatched up her keys and dashed out the door. Maggie jumped behind the wheel of her car and drove to the bakery in Marietta. Finding a parking spot, she hopped out the car making her way towards the entrance and stopped dead in her tracks at the sight before her. As she watched Camilla and Rafiq kiss and hug each other in front of the shop, her blood began to boil. She was unaware that two of them linked back up with each other but for her daughter to be with him while her husband was the middle of a crisis infuriated her.

"Camilla Hayes-Jacobs, what the hell do you think you're doing." She pulled them a part.

"Mom, what the hell are you doing here?"

"I came here to talk to you since I haven't seen you in months and then I find you kissing this no-good hoodlum!" She shouted.

"Hoodlum?" Rafiq chuckled, "You know what Miss Maggie, I'm not gonna get into it with you right now. Just know our time will come." He kissed Camilla's cheek and headed to his car.

The women watched him drive off before Maggie spoke again.

"What the fuck are you doing with him!" She pulled him to the side. "Your *husband* is in the middle of a damn scandal and your ass is out here running around with that damn thug!" she whispered in a hushed tone.

"I don't give a damn if Kane is in a damn scandal," Camilla shouted in a hushed tone, "The fact that this story leaked is working in my favor. From this public humiliation, I have so many people on my side. My customers are showing me empathy, giving me well wishes and other positive vibes. Kane has disrespected me for the last time, and I will not stand by him through this shit."

"Camilla, you are making a huge mistake. That man loves you."

"Well I tell you what, mama, since you seem to be team Kane, how about you ride for him then." She pushed past her mom, making her stumble.

"Wait a damn minute." She walked back over to Maggie. "How the hell do you know Rafiq?"

"What do you mean?"

"He called you by name, mom. He said that y'all time will

come. Why would he say that? What did you do?" Camilla shouted.

"I make it my business to know everyone you come in contact with and let's just leave it at that." Maggie stared at her.

The two women stared at each other for a moment before Camilla spoke.

"I don't know what you've done or what you did but you better hope I don't find out about it." She warned before heading back into the bakery.

Feeling disrespected, Maggie was about to go after her daughter until she saw that the truck that Rafiq pulled off in riding back down the street. She quickly hopped behind the wheel of her car, brought it to life and made an illegal U-turn in the middle of the street. Maggie ignored the blaring horns as she drove down the street like a bat out of hell. Catching up to the truck, Maggie stepped on the gas driving next to it. She was about to tell who she thought was Rafiq to pull over but when she got a glimpse at the driver, she lost sight of the road and drove through the intersection. Swerving out the way avoiding an 18-wheeler, Maggie pulled over to the side of the road to calm herself down. A few minutes later, her phone began to ring and she jumped with fear. Maggie removed her phone from her purse and even though the number was private, she still answered.

"Hello," she greeted with a shaky voice.

"Why do I have to call you from a blocked number in order for you to answer my calls," the man's deep, husky voice boomed through the phone.

"I..I didn't know that was you calling me."

"What? After all we've been through. You don't have my number saved anymore?"

"When did you get back in town?"

"A couple of weeks ago. We have a few things we need to discuss Maggie. I need to see you soon."

"No. I don't want anything to do with you anymore." She fought back tears.

"If I gave you the impression that you had a choice, I didn't mean to. Now when I text you with a time and location, you better be there because if you choose not to show, that husband of yours is going to find out about our relationship once and for all."

When the call ended, Maggie broke out in tears as she thought about how her world was falling apart. She knew that it was only a matter of time before Rafiq told Camilla everything she had done to him and now that Richard was hearing things about her, she knew it was only a matter of time before they discovered the truth about her. Being the scheme artist that she was, Maggie's mind began to race as she thought of a way to get out of the mess she was in. Up until that point, the only person Maggie cared about was herself. She was willing to destroy anyone that stood in her way, including her own husband. Although she was a lousy wife and mother for the past two years, she still cared for her husband and daughter very much and she was positive that they weren't going to want Maggie in their lives once they learned the truth about her. So, she was going to do everything in her power to live the best life she could until her secrets were revealed.

## 22

As Camilla continued with her work day, she found it hard to concentrate on her duties. She couldn't shake her thoughts of the brief exchange of words between Rafiq and Maggie. She tried her hardest to recall if she ever mentioned Rafiq to her parents and Camilla's mind drew a blank. Her mother's words of how she made it her business to know everyone that was in Camilla's life stood out in a daunting way. Thinking back to her childhood, Maggie always viewed the kids that she hung out with as hood rats, ghetto and thugs but Camilla never chilled around boys where her parents could see her. She always linked up with them outside of her neighborhood and the only boys she chilled with on a daily basis were Boyce and Rafiq. She always made sure to cover to her tracks so she was confused as to when and how Maggie find out about Rafiq.

As Camilla finished up with a customer, she swept the floor before she began mopping it. She caught a few stares from the customers that were coming into the store and wondered why they were staring at her, but she ignored them and kept mopping.

"Uh, C? Are you aight?" Nakia spoke from behind the counter.

"Yeah. Why?"

"Because I always thought you needed water to mop but your bucket is empty." She turned the empty bucket upside down.

"Damn. No wonder why the customers were staring at me like I was the fuck crazy." Camilla shook her head before flopping down in one of the chairs. "I'm tripping for real."

"What's going on sis? Is it this situation with Kane?"

"Nah. I'm not tripping about that. Simply because due to this act of public humiliation, I'm finally gonna get my divorce. I knew Kane wasn't gonna sign the papers at the private meeting I set up at my parents' house and I was wondering how I was gonna convince him to sign them but I don't have to worry about that now."

"I'm sorry you're going through this, C. You don't deserve to be going through no shit like this even if it is working out in your favor," Nakia sincerely spoke, "So if you ain't tripping off Kane, what got ya mind gone?"

"When I walked Rafiq to his car earlier, my mom pulled us apart and called him a hoodlum. Rafiq told my mom that their time will come and I've been having the toughest time trying to figure out how the fuck they know each other," Camilla honestly answered.

Noticing the expression on her besties face, she knew that Nakia knew something.

"Wassup, Nakia?" She questioned with a raised eye brow.

"Nothing, Camilla. Nothing at all." Nakia quickly stood to her feet walking behind the counter.

"Your lying, Kia." Camilla followed her. "You know something." She pointed at her.

"Camilla," she sighed, "I really would like to tell you but I'm afraid that if I do, you're not gonna believe me." Her expression changed from guilty to worry.

"What? Why would I not believe you," she asked confused, "Nakia, what's going on?"

"Me, Boyce and Rafiq were gonna sit you down and have this conversation with you when we had our facts straight, but I guess we can talk about this now."

Nakia took a deep breath before speaking.

"About a week ago, two detectives showed up at my house asking about Rafiq and when he arrived at our house, the detectives told him that the people who framed him are singing like canaries, and they mentioned that a woman was the mastermind behind their scheme. Then...they showed...us a picture...of your mother," Nakia solemnly spoke.

"My mother! You lying!" she shouted in disbelief.

"I wish I was, Camilla."

With a shocked expression plastered on Camilla's face, she tried to wrap her mind around what her friend was telling her.

"There's more, Camilla. Rafiq told the detectives that Maggie tried to bribe him with a number of things to get him to leave you alone, but he never took anything she offered him. She was so determined to get Rafiq outta the way, she set him up, causing him to spend six years of his life in prison."

"I can't believe this shit!"

"C, I know that this is a lot to handle right now but I'm not finished yet."

"No, Nakia. You are finished!" she marched to the back gathering her things. "I know my mother has her issues, but she wouldn't do no shit like that to anybody! And for you to make up some shit like that about my mother is pathetic!"

"Hold the fuck up! Now I may not like your mother but I damn sure wouldn't lie on her or anybody for that damn matter! I knew you weren't gonna be able to handle the fucking truth about your mama which is why I didn't wanna tell you in the first place!" Nakia shouted. "Your mother done cause Rafiq to lose out on six years of his life and she might be the one who killed my fucking mother in law as well!"

"Why the fuck would my mother kill Jackie? That shit doesn't make any fucking sense, so I know you're lying now!"

"Maggie might've killed Jackie because she was the one working so hard so get Rafiq outta jail and to stop her from doing so, she killed my damn mother in law! Your mother done fucked with my family for the last time and who knows how many other people she done fucked over! Maggie is a fucked-up individual and you better believe that she's gonna pay for what the fuck she did to my family!"

The women stared each other down with hatred burning in their eyes and Camilla's rage was on the rise. It was one thing for Nakia to stand there telling lies about her mother but for her to threaten Maggie was taking shit to the next level.

"I don't appreciate you threatening my mother and for you to do so lets me know where I stand with you Nakia. I never thought that our friendship would ever end again but I guess I was wrong."

Giving her a quick glance over, Camilla turned on her heels and headed out the door power walking to her car. She tossed her things in the passenger seat then got behind the wheel, starting the engine and pulling off in the direction of Kannon's summer camp. Her blood was still boiling from the argument she had with Nakia but besides being angry, she was also hurt. She couldn't understand why her best friend would say some foul shit like that about Maggie and the longer she pondered about the situation, the more it made Camilla wonder if Nakia was telling lies about her mother or not. Nakia was the one to tell her that her parents' might have secrets that they were trying to keep under wraps and she couldn't help but to think that this was one of those secrets but before she believed that her mother was the conniving bitch her bestie made her out to be, Camilla needed to get some answers on her own.

Arriving twenty minutes later, Camilla signed her son out of camp, taking him by the hand and guiding him out the door. As she strapped Kannon in his seat, a deep familiar voice called her name from behind her instantly getting her attention.

"Kane! What the fuck are you doing here?"

"I came here to get my wife and son," he deviously smirked.

"What you mean you came to get us?" Her heart pounded out of her chest.

"My life has been turned upside in the matter of days. My reputation is ruined, and I've been called every type of name in the damn book for having an outside kid on my wife. I know you don't give a fuck about me but I'm still in love with you and I'm not leaving here without you and my son Camilla," Kane spoke calmly.

"Well I guess this is gonna be your new home because we're not coming home with you," She stated with disgust.

Walking around to the driver side, Camilla felt something hard poking her in the back paralyzing her with fear.

"This ain't up for debate Camilla," Kane aggressively whispered in her ear. "Now if you don't get the fuck in this car and drive to the mansion, I will kill you and Kannon right here in broad daylight. Now what the fuck is it gonna be?

Without hesitation, Camilla got in her car, pulling into traffic as she headed towards the expressway. Tears rolled down her cheeks as she drove, and she tried to keep her sobbing low so her son couldn't hear her. Camilla was scared shitless of Kane and what he would do to them if she didn't obey his wishes. The fact that he threatened to kill not only her, but their son as well let her know that Kane wasn't playing with a full deck of cards. After working so hard to escape the sheltered life that he provided her, Camilla hated that she was being forced to return to it, but in order to protect her son from the monster that was his father, she didn't have a choice. There was no way in hell that she was going to stay with the man that made her life miserable, but Camilla prayed that her and Kannon would be able to get away from Kane alive instead of being buried.

**TO BE CONTINUED...**

# AUTHOR'S NOTES

Thank you for taking the time to read the first installment of my new series, Married to the Boss of Atlanta. I hope you enjoyed reading it as much as I enjoyed writing it. If this is your first time reading anything from me, I hope I have gained a new fan and for those who have supported me through my journey, I pray that you will continue to support me in the future. If you have ever done anything to support me on my journey, whether it was share a post, change your picture to my book cover, shared the link to my book, brainstormed with me or test read any of my work for me, just know that I truly appreciate you and all you do. Part 2 to this series will be coming soon. I hope you're ready because it's going to be a wild ride. (LOL)

## OTHER BOOKS BY DANI LITTLEPAGE:

All Eyes on Us 1-3

Just Like the Rest of Em 1&2

My Other Babymama 1-3

Fallin' for a Philly Boss

Issa Hood Love Story: Carlee & Macklin

Hoodwives and Rich Thugs of Houston 1&2

Thug Holiday 1-5

The Rock Boyz 1-3

Baby Mama Drama

Diamond & Boss 1&2

I Gave My Heart to a A-Town Thug

CPSIA information can be obtained
at www.ICGtesting.com
Printed in the USA
LVHW041946061120
670968LV00003B/477